Something Old, Something New...

A novel by

Erica N. Martin

Something Old, Something New...

A Second Media & Communications Book/Published by Arrangement with the author(s): Erica N. Martin

Printing History
First Printing: May 2009

For information:
Second Time Media & Communications
P.O. Box 401367
Redford, MI 48240-1367
www.2ndtimeonline.net

ISBN: 978-0-9840660-0-1

Printed in the United States of America

Dedication

One thing I've learned over the years is that sometimes life is stranger than fiction. I live my life like there is no tomorrow, for I know tomorrow isn't promised. This book is dedicated to the "Carter" in my life.

If I had no more minutes in this life to live, I would want you to know that you came into my life and changed me for the better. You have made each day more meaningful because I spend them with you. You challenge me to be better and show me by example how to be stronger.

I admire your courage, your spirituality, your desire to seek knowledge and challenge what the masses are led to believe. I'm inspired by your courage to reach beyond the unknown. Your tenacity to excel encourages me.

Every day I spend with you is like a new adventure. The laughter that rings through our home is contagious and everyone that comes around us is infected. You know me like you know yourself so you accept me, flaws and all. You've shown me love like I've never known and I thank you for showing me that forever more...belongs to us. This book is dedicated to my husband, Greg O. Jones.

P.S. Thanks for your contributions to this masterpiece!

Gary and Mookie everything I do, I do for you. You both make my heart sing. You both make Mommie proud and I strive every day to make you proud of me. I love you both.

" Whoso findeth a wife, findeth a good thing" Proverbs 18:22

Part I

Something Old...Something New

Chapter 1

"Baby, I really think this is a bad idea. You've been up all day and you know you can't drive at night," Audrey said as she watched her fiancé Carter get up out of their bed.

As he switched on the vintage desk lamp atop of the computer desk, an eerie glow cast over the previously darkened room. His masculine features became visible as he searched the floor for the jogging pants he had discarded just a mere hour before.

She loved watching him. Over the course of two and a half years she had grown to love everything about him. That night was different though. She hoped that the look of discernment on her face would penetrate his stubbornness but to no avail, he proceeded to pull down the wife beater t-shirt over his muscular chest indicating that he still intended to go on the impromptu road trip with his best friend Mike, despite the worry in her eyes.

She sat up in the king-sized bed planning to take one more stab at convincing him to stay. The huge bed seemed to swallow her little frame. At 5'2, 120 lbs, she looked like a little kid in the bed.

"Carter? Are you listening to me?"

"Hmm? Yeah, baby," he said as he answered the buzzing phone on his hip. Audrey impatiently listened to Carter's side of the conversation.

"Hello. Yeah...man, you sure you don't want to wait until the morning? I'm kinda tired, unless you want to start out driving."

Audrey's false sense of hope was immediately dashed as Carter agreed to 'thug it out' with his friend to pick up a car that he was buying from a private owner in Chicago.

She laid down in defeat and snuggled under the down comforter as he came and sat on her side of the bed. He really didn't want to go but always the loyal friend, he sometimes pushed himself to the limit.

He caressed her face, and she turned away with an attitude.

"I can't believe you are still going to go," she whined with her back turned to him. "It's 1:30 in the morning. The roads are icy and you both are tired. Are you really going to get up out of *our* bed to go on this stupid mission?"

"Baby, I promise I'll be ok. We're going straight down and coming back up. I'll be back before you get off work," he explained while pulling her shoulder so she would face him.

Reluctantly, she faced the love of her life and gave in. His promise was always absolute with Audrey. Carter cherished his wife to be and meant every endearing word he gave her. Promises were one of the things he never took for granted in their relationship.

She grabbed his shirt and pulled him down to her. He lied next to her and she playfully yet seriously unbuttoned his shirt as a last ditch effort to get him to stay. Carter then, more playfully than seriously, moved her hands and buttoned back up his shirt. He leaned up from the bed and stared deeply into her worried eyes.

In a more serious and direct tone of compassion, Carter promised, "I'll be back before you even get a chance to miss me, okay? You know I gotta get back to my baby." He reached in and kissed her lips. The electricity from their kiss transferred over into the insistent buzzing of his cell phone. Defeated, she released his face from her cupped hands.

"I gotta go baby...he's waiting on me," Carter said sincerely.

She held on to the sleeve of his pea coat as he rose to make his descent down the stairs.

"When you get back we need to talk about caterers, okay? You promised me you would go cake sampling with me," Audrey shouted softly. Her words chased him down the steps.

"So you already know it's a done deal then, right?" he yelled back up the stairs.

"I love you," she said sincerely as she clutched the pillow he had momentarily slept on. The scent of his body sent chills up her spine.

"I love you more," Carter whispered loudly just as he hit the bottom step.

"No you don't buddy..." she said into the darkness. She turned on her back from her side as she lay alone in the quiet room. Audrey let out a huge sigh as she heard the thud of the front door closing behind him. She held up the 3 carat round solitaire diamond on her left hand and smiled. That was her pacification until he returned; the thought of marrying the man of her dreams.

She jumped up because she knew she would never be able to fall right to sleep. There were a ton of things that she still had to do in preparation for the big day. Even though it was mid November and the wedding wasn't until next year in September, there was so much planning to do and she intended on making Carter do his part.

He was so mild mannered that whatever she liked he agreed with. But they were a team and besides, she loved spending time with him. She wrote some things on her "Honey-do" list and then went downstairs to the kitchen for a bottle of Evian. As she passed through the hallway, her nose was met with the scent of the dozen red and white roses that he had given her earlier.

The red and white symbols of love and purity stood regally in the center of the cherry oak and smoked glass table. They had blossomed since she had arranged them and put them in water. Their beauty only reminded her of him and how much he really loved her.

Audrey smiled at the shenanigans that he had gone through to surprise her. All day long he had made himself scarce saying that he and Mike had decided to take the road trip early to pick up the car and of course she believed him. He even went so far as to make her a little mad by not answering his phone. Then, just as she was getting ready to go to show a house, he called and told her to pick up a package for him at the clinic that he was working at. With an attitude she raced to the clinic so that Jenny, the receptionist could leave for the day.

"Hey Jenny, is there a package here for Carter?" Audrey asked the fresh-faced receptionist.

"No…but there is a package here for you," she said pulling out the beautiful flowers.

"Awww! He is such a jerk!" she said picking up the bouquet and smelling them.

Suddenly she felt his strong arms around her waist.

"Surprise!" he said smiling down at her.

He had tricked her into believing that he was already gone and had been in the city all day, setting her up for this surprise.

As she stood in front of the beautiful flowers on top of the cherry oak table, she had wished with all her heart that he was cajoling her again.

Audrey's thoughts of that day were interrupted by her matron of honor, Shauntel who was knocking on the door to the private dressing room reserved for the bride. Shauntel's knocks brought her back to present day in which she would finally be walking down the aisle in a few hours.

"Hey Audrey, I was checking in with the wedding planner. Everything is all set and it's starting to look really beautiful out there," Shauntel expressed with a huge grin. She hung the garment bag up that held her dress and smiled when she saw the beautiful gown that her best friend in the whole wide world would soon be wearing. She walked over to the vanity where Audrey sat at looking in the mirror. "Hey, why are you crying?"

"I was just thinking about the last time I..."

Audrey's sentence was cut off with, "Oh honey, don't cry! This is going to be a beautiful day. Besides, you know you look like Madea when you cry."

Shauntel's tactic worked. Audrey burst out laughing through her tears and pulled up a photo album as Shauntel scanned the room for some napkins to dab away the watery emotions on Audrey's eyelids.

"I was looking through these pi-pic...pictures of us...," the rest of the words were caught in her throat as she looked down at the picture of Carter, herself, Shauntel and Shauntel's husband, Kyle.

Shauntel sat on the ottoman at the chaise next to the bride and looked down at the picture she was stuck on. Seeing the picture brought Shauntel to tears as well.

"Am I doing the right thing Shaunie? Am I really ready for this?" Audrey muffled through the tears.

Shauntel looked at her friend and with assurance said, "Of course you are sweetie. This has truly been a long time coming and you of all people deserve it." She nudged Audrey in the side. "He is a wonderful man, and might I add *'fine as hell'*, and you guys are going to live happily ever after!"

Shauntel rubbed her best friend's back as she strolled down memory lane recalling the first time she and her husband were introduced to Carter…

"You're going to love him. I've never met anyone like him Shauntel," Audrey gushed into the phone.

"Well, if he's anything like you say he is, you know I will. So we'll meet you guys at Dave and Busters in an hour."

An hour later Shauntel was scanning the room for her best friend and new beau in tow. For Audrey to sing this man's praises as she had was a feat in itself.

Audrey was a commitment phobe. At the slightest indication of someone wanting a commitment, she would run the other way. It wasn't just with dating; Shauntel could barely get her to commit to a lunch date if it was too far in advance. After suffering through a few bad relationships Shauntel could hardly blame her. Audrey had her heart under lock and key but somehow this man had gained access.

Shauntel could barely hear herself think as the music blared around her. Bells were ringing as people competed at skeeball where she and her husband stood. Laughter and the overall feeling of happiness were all around them. Shauntel picked up her phone to dial Audrey's number when all of a sudden; her husband did something rather unusual.

Kyle, a self considered alpha male was never the one to be fond of PDA's (public displays of affection). But suddenly, he slid his arm around Shauntel's waist and pulled her closer to him. She paused in the middle of her hissy fit and wondered what the hell had gotten into Kyle. As she looked him in the face for a quick explanation, she immediately spotted the real reason for his display of affection. There was a gorgeous man walking in the door of the family entertainment center.

He stood at an even 6'2 with the body of an Olympic swimmer. Anyone could tell he took care of his body. His caramel complexion was flawless and the deep dimples on each side of his perfectly lined smile only complimented even more his strikingly good looks. His wavy black hair was cut low in a Caesar cut and his mustache and goatee were impeccably trimmed. He was nothing short of magnificent.

Shauntel cleared her throat and quickly shifted her eyes and attention from the Adonis of a man before her husband of three years caught her staring too long.

"Shauntel! Kyle! Over here," Audrey yelled across the room.

They both followed her voice and were surprised to see her standing with the guy that they both had so seemingly noticed.

"Hey girl," Shauntel said giving Audrey a more intense than usual hug.

"Hey Boozer," Audrey said as she playfully punched Kyle in the shoulder before opening up her arms for a hug from him. 'Boozer' was Kyle's childhood nickname. They had known each other since elementary school and Audrey had hooked Shauntel and Kyle up years ago.

"Audrey, Kyle, this is Carter," she said proudly trying to mask the excitement inside.

"Ok, ok...that's good we all know each other's government name, but my question is, "Who is ready to get their butts kicked in the basketball shoot out?" Carter jabbed at the trio.

"Aww, hell naw dawg! She didn't tell you that I'm the hoop city king?" Kyle shot back.

"Well let's do this then," Carter said as he dropped Audrey's hand and began stretching and cracking his knuckles. "You ready playa...meet me at the court!" Carter led the way as he walked swiftly over to the basketball game, choosing which side he would shoot from first. The ladies looked at each other and shook their heads.

With the girls in tow, Audrey turned to Shauntel and said, "Let's show them who really runs this!" They hi-fived each other and took their places in front of the next two available basketball rims.

Four games later both of the men had quit and Audrey and Shauntel were playing the final tie breaker as they each had won two games each.

After four hours of Dance Nation, Skeeball, Bowling, Air Hockey, more basketball and the trivia game, the group was thoroughly exhausted. They settled in at the bar and had a late dinner.

It was there that Shauntel noticed the most intriguing physical attribute about Carter...his eyes. The way he looked at Audrey said it all. There was nothing but love in his eyes as he gazed at her. It was almost as if he was in awe of her. She watched from across the table at how giddy Audrey was and smiled as the two love birds shared their own private jokes. This man had to be a God to have her best friend behaving like this. Shauntel knew at that very moment that this man was going to be Audrey's husband...

"Yeah, I remember that day like yesterday. He was so in love with you. I could see it all in his eyes. His love was always in his eyes for you from the first day." Shauntel went on with the rest of the story as the two of them lost track of time reminiscing.

Carter and Kyle had become good friends and the two couples did a lot together. They'd taken a trip every summer since they'd met.

"Remember the Cancun trip?" Shauntel asked.

"Yeah, when I was going to have to go upside that tramp's head?" Audrey said.

"Girl, she was fooling though," Shauntel replied shamelessly.

They had been in Cancun for a day enjoying the beautiful weather and relaxing. They were scheduled to go horseback riding and were waiting at the stable when one of the female guides took a very aggressive interest in Carter. She had made her way over to the group and asked if Carter would mind helping her move a trough that was too heavy for her. This request got raised eyebrows from Shauntel and Audrey but Kyle, who seemed to be admiring the backside view as the guide struggled to carry the trough, didn't think anything of it.

"Maybe she should go get someone who works here Carter. You're on vacation, "Shauntel suggested flatly.

Carter, always the perfect gentleman replied, "It's not a problem. Let me move that for you," he said grabbing the trough.

"Yeah, let me help you out Bro," Kyle said grabbing the other handle on the trough.

Both Audrey and Shauntel stood there with puzzled looks on their faces. Shauntel directed Kyle back immediately with a nasty and disapproving look. Audrey, on the other hand, sucked her teeth as she retreated back to the gate.

The perky senorita soon realized that she may have won the fight but quickly lost the war as Carter joined his fiancé and kissed her square on the lips. He then stood behind her and held her tightly by the waist, in plain view for the senorita to see, acknowledging Audrey's place. He didn't so much as glance back at the now pouting chick.

Audrey smiled as she thought back to that moment.

"That's much better. I need to see more smiles and less tears, Audrey," Shauntel said passing her another piece of Kleenex. "This is your special day sweetie. Let me make some phone calls and see where the rest of the girls are."

Audrey smiled at her friend. Shauntel was right. This was a very special day, a day that had been a long time coming.

Chapter 2

The ladies were interrupted by a tap at the door. Shauntel walked over to see who it was. She prayed it wasn't the groom as she knew he would be anxious to see Audrey. She slowly opened the door and was almost knocked down by Alyssa, Audrey's older sister who burst in.

"Hey ladies! It's just me," Alyssa screamed in her usual boisterous manner before she noticed the two girls were crying. "Oh no, what's wrong baby?" she asked in a much softer tone as she placed her belongings on the couch and slid onto the ottoman that Shauntel had previously occupied.

Though caught up in concern for her sister, Alyssa couldn't help but notice the elaborate layout of the mega-mansion they were getting married in. The dressing room that they sat in was three rooms combined in her house combined. Alyssa was the oldest of the three children. Audrey was the middle child and Austin was their younger brother.

"She's going down memory lane," Shauntel said pointing to the open photo album on the vanity. After Carter had expressed interest in photography, Audrey had gone out and bought him a Sony Alpha state-of-the-art camera, and he'd gone wild with it. He took pictures all the time.

The photo album had fallen open to a photo of the happy couple on a picnic. Alyssa looked at the album which was beautifully crafted. She turned to the first page and noticed the pictures were set in chronological order. She ran her fingers across a picture of Audrey and Carter at a black tie benefit dinner for the Humane Society.

"That was our first 'date'," Audrey said running her slender finger over the photo. "We didn't even know each other."

Audrey had always promised to volunteer her time to at least one charitable cause and that year it had been at the Humane Society. She worked a few hours a month at the adoption drives that they held monthly and had been personally invited to the benefit dinner by the Director at the shelter in which she was volunteering.

She didn't have a date and felt so awkward standing outside the Gallery that they were holding the extravagant ordeal at. She was lucky that she could still squeeze into the gown that she had bought from Parisians a few months before. After going on a Bon-Bon diet from breaking up with some guy whose name she couldn't even remember now, she had put on a few pounds.

She stood there looking up the 26 (yes, she had counted) stairs to reach the entrance. She noticed the many couples filing into the benefit and felt so out of place. She had just decided to turn around and go back home when she bumped into someone standing behind her with his back to hers.

"Oh, I'm sorry," she said staring into the eyes of the most handsome man she had ever laid eyes on.

"No, please. I'm sorry. I wasn't watching where I was going. As a matter of fact I was turning around to leave," he said nervously with a smile.

"Me too," she remarked incredulously.

"You were leaving, too? Don't you have to wait on your date?" he asked presumptuously.

"That's why I'm leaving," she replied meekly, careful to keep her eyes leveled with the ground. "I don't have a date." She excused herself and turned to walk back to her car.

"Ms.? Ma'am?" he called as he jogged to catch up with her. "I know this is going to sound crazy but that's the same reason I was leaving," he said gently grabbing her forearm to stop her from walking. His touch sent shots of electricity through her body. "Again, this might sound crazy but why don't we go together and solve both of our problems."

"Are you asking me out on a date?" she said wearing a devilish smile.

"Well, I guess I am. It would be nice to know who I'm dating though. My name is Carter. Carter Bradford," he said extending his hand.

"Audrey. Audrey Parchman," she replied shaking his hand.

"Shall we?" he asked offering his folded arm for her to hold on to.

They immediately hit it off. They had so many things in common and there were hardly any gaps in the conversation.

There was a photographer capturing the event for the Society and he snapped a picture of them dancing. After the song ended, the photographer showed them the picture and agreed to send them a copy. The picture showed Carter holding Audrey close with her head lying on his chest. The couple looked so in love. They danced all night until the last partygoers besides them were leaving.

At the end of the night, neither of them wanted the night to end...so it didn't. Carter stayed the night at Audrey's house and they had been inseparable ever since.

The two of them may have walked into the Gallery as strangers but strolled out together as soul mates...

"The ultimate love story," Alyssa said smiling at her sister. "This union is what great romance novels are made of," she said pointing at the picture.

Audrey smiled at the comment Alyssa made. She moved from the vanity and walked across the room to the private bathroom adjacent to the sitting area.

"How is she?" Alyssa asked Shauntel who had taken a seat on the Victorian styled Chaise Lounge. The room was decorated in soft tans and crèmes and the drapes were made of lace. The sunshine streamed through the tall windows and cast a rainbow of light into the room.

"She's okay. You know how tough this is for her. She asked me if I thought she was ready and of course I told her she was. She has what every woman has always dreamed of having; a man that adores her and would do anything to make her happy. She needs to take this step forward," Shauntel explained.

Alyssa flipped the page of the album and was drawn to a picture of herself, her twins Raquel and Raphael, Audrey and Carter at Cedar Pointe. That photo took her back to one of the hardest times in her life. She remembered making that initial phone call…

"Audrey?"

"Alyssa? What's wrong? Where are you?" Audrey asked sitting up in the bed. She immediately heard the desperation in her sister's voice and shook Carter to wake him.

"I'm at the house. He…he is putting us out," she cried into the phone.

"What?! How the hell is he putting *you* out? You pay the damn bills over there," Audrey said pulling the covers back and jumping out of the bed. Carter quickly followed suit because he was more than pissed by what he had just heard.

"Audrey, it doesn't matter. I need to get away from here anyway. I'm tired of this. He's drinking again and the kids don't need to be exposed to..." she stopped short of finishing the sentence.

Audrey stopped in her tracks. "Is he hitting you?"

Before Alyssa could answer Carter had grabbed the phone. "Get your shit together. We're on our way to get you and the kids, now!"

The couple threw on whatever clothing was at hand and raced over to the house in the middle class neighborhood that her sister had worked so hard to maintain. As a middle school teacher Alyssa wasn't making much money and when her husband, Rocky had been laid off from General Motors, she assumed all the responsibility of taking care of the household as he resigned to drinking himself into a stupor.

Audrey had a strong suspicion that Rocky had hit Alyssa once or twice but Alyssa would never admit to it. She was a prideful woman and had never really shared her business with anyone other than Audrey.

Alyssa also knew that Carter was a direct extension of Audrey and anything she told Audrey would eventually trickle its way down to Carter.

When they pulled up to the house, Carter was out of the car faster than Audrey. He crossed the poorly manicured lawn in long strides. Audrey ran behind him. Carter rang the bell and Audrey braced herself for what was to come. She'd only known Carter for six months at that time but she knew that there were things that he had no tolerance for and domestic violence was one.

His mother had been beaten by his step-father and he'd seen plenty of abused women come through the clinic where he worked. Carter was totally against any man hitting a woman. He'd heard the stories of how no good Rocky was and had even tried to talk Alyssa into seeking some counseling, to which she refused. But this was the final straw. It would be an injustice for him to keep silent this time. Alyssa wasn't just Audrey's sister, she was his family, too.

After the third ring of the doorbell with no answer, Carter pounded on the wooden door with his tightened fist. Before the door swung upon, he heard some bustling on the other side of the door. That incited Carter even more. He raised his foot and was just about to launch a menacing thrust when Rocky snatched the door open. He looked a mess and staggered through the foyer.

Carter forcefully stepped in behind him and sternly asked for Alyssa's whereabouts.

"Don't know, don't give a damn. Man, who do you think you are anyway asking me questions in my house, pretty boy?"

Rocky was testing Carter. Carter's patience was at zero and he was about to answer him with a choke slam when Audrey stepped in and asked for Alyssa.

"Where is my sister?" Audrey said pushing past the drunken man.

"She better be getting her shit together," Rocky slurred. "Hey, and next time you bring a mut pretendin' to be a tiger, keep him on a fuckin' leash. It would be a shame to have to put him down..."

That comment was aimed directly at Carter as Rocky took another swig at his liquor and stared him down. Carter's thoughts were faster than his reactions as he imagined Rocky between his grips squeezing the life out of him. Instead, Carter clenched his jaws and allowed Audrey to handle it.

She stopped and turned back to him, "You fucking pig. You ought to be ashamed of yourself." She proceeded up the stairs where she could hear her sister walking around.

Carter stood in the threshold of the doorway staring at Rocky in disgust. It was evident that his mild mannered temper was about to blow from the frown on his face.

Rocky stammered from one wall to the next as he laughed to himself about the whole situation.

"I just need to know one thing. Did you put your hands on her?" Carter growled through his clenched teeth.

"So I guess you must be that bitch's savior, huh?"

Carter didn't respond. Instead, he turned to the steps and informed Audrey and her sister to please hurry before something really bad happens.

"Oh, so what you sayin' pretty boy? You tough? You think you tough or something? And you standin' in my mutha fuckin' house? Pretty boy, looka here...go back to your girlfriend's house and play with her, don't come in my house playin' wit me! All that starin' and shit ain't gon win you nuthin' but a free ass whoopin, momma's boy!"

Audrey and Alyssa were coming down the stairs when the end of Rocky's sentence came out. Audrey knew Carter would lose it after hearing that as she tried to rush down to prevent the imminent.

Before Rocky could finish his vile sentence Carter threw his forearm under Rocky's chin and pushed him up against the wall.

Carter towered over Rocky as his feet kicked and scraped the wall six inches up. They were face to face now as Carter pulled him up with the death grip that he had locked in on his neck. No words were spoken, just Rocky choking and sputtering as Carter applied more pressure. Audrey and Alyssa ran down the stairs just as Carter was reeling back to punch Rocky in the face.

"Carter, please... he's not worth it," Alyssa said in a calming voice.

Audrey stepped in and placed her hand on Carter's back in attempts to idle his anger.

"Baby, don't. The kids are upstairs. We're ready to go. Just let him go," Audrey coaxed him.

Carter stared into the eyes of the injured coward and said, "If you ever come near them again, I promise you, on everything I love, I *will* kill you." Carter snatched back his forearm that was firmly pressed against Rocky's throat and walked away. Rocky fell flat on his hands and knees gasping for air.

"Y-you threatening me?" he managed to spit out between coughs.

Carter swiveled around swiftly and fired back, "Try me, and you'll see you worthless piece of..."

Audrey interjected Carter before he could finish his sentence. "Baby, it's done, okay?"

She stood in between the standing Carter and the kneeling Rocky. Still pumped with anger, Carter lowered his eyes to Audrey's and found calmness. She kept her eyes steady on her man, convincing him that the altercation was over and that Rocky wasn't worth the energy.

They gathered up all they could fit into the two cars and Alyssa and the twins came to live with them until she was the in the position to get a place.

Alyssa had to dab at her eyes as she thought of how Carter and Audrey had helped save her life. Shauntel rubbed her shoulders because she was familiar with the story and though it was two years before Alyssa was still trying to move past it all.

She and the kids had been living with Audrey and Carter for two weeks when he surprised them all with a trip to an amusement park. Alyssa had planned on doing laundry and tying up loose ends that Saturday morning. She was surprised when the crazy couple and the twins came jumping on her bed at 6 o'clock in the morning.

"We're going to Cedar Pointe!" they all screamed.

Alyssa could barely wipe the sleep from her eyes before the house was in total mayhem. Showers were running, breakfast was being packed and she unwillingly had been swept right into the middle of the chaos.

They arrived at the amusement park just after 8'oclock and they rushed to the gates to beat the rest of the thrill seekers. They stayed from sun up to sun down and Alyssa got some much needed joy in her life...

"Girl, he spent over fifty dollars trying to win that damn parrot for her," Alyssa laughed pointing to the huge life sized bird in the picture. "The kid that was running the booth felt so bad for him that when Audrey turned her back, he let him pay him for it!"

"That's typical Carter. Her every wish is his command," Shauntel said just as Audrey walked out of the bathroom.

"Getting to you too, huh?" Audrey said walking back into the room. She had grabbed the plush bath robe from the spacious bathroom and wrapped it around her body.

"Oh, Audrey look!" gasped Shauntel and waving for Audrey to hurry. "Remember this one?!! You two were so cute together!"

Audrey pouted and dragged her feet as she moved closer to the picture album. "Come on you guys, that's enough, okay? I get the hint and I feel better now. You know I have to get ready before Inga..." She couldn't whine another word when her eyes locked on a picture of her and Carter.

As the girls continued to flip through the book, Audrey stood stoic as the picture brought back fresh memories.

"No wait, go back to that picture," instructed Audrey as she had to take a closer look of it. Audrey removed the picture from up underneath its transparent film and found a seat alone by the white baby grand piano.

"I remember how nervous he was that day. He couldn't even sleep the night before," thought Audrey as she looked off into a corner of the room with a genuine oak grandfather clock standing adjacent to the portraits of the owners of the mansion that they were in...

"Carter, why are you still up?" questioned Audrey as he steadily paced their bedroom floor.

"I-I can't sleep babe, I don't know. I guess I'm all nervous and excited at the same time. Wh-what would you call that?"

Audrey yawned and said, "I would call it nervo-excitis, if I had to diagnose you!"

Carter smiled then ducked as a pillow came flying in his direction.

"Come on honey, come back to bed...besides, I think I found the cure for your ailment already."

She stood up and removed her top. Carter's pacing quickly ended after seeing her nude frame.

"Now, even though you're going to be a doctor tomorrow, I think I need a physical tonight." Audrey twisted her body from one side to the next then pointed her finger at Carter. "Come here...doc. I've got a pain down low."

Carter grabbed hold of her small waist and began kissing and licking her navel. Audrey removed her hair scarf and held her hair up above her head with both hands, enjoying his every touch.

Cupping her buttocks, Carter lifted Audrey from the bed as she let her hair fall to her face and wrapped her arms around his neck. The two made love and for the first time in their relationship, had unprotected sex.

Carter grabbed his camera off the nightstand as Audrey slept on his chest. He stared down at her and snapped the picture unbeknownst to her.

The morning light shined through the blinds and danced on Audrey's face, awaking her from the continued feeling of elation from just a couple of hours ago.

Stretching, she noticed Carter wasn't in the bed with her. Turning over and waiting for her eyes to adjust, she found a note attached to a flower beside her.

It read: For the first time, we shared each other without interference and inhibitions, hopefully our love made will make life..."

Audrey was misty–eyed after reading the precious note. Carter was a very sentimental guy and she adored the sensitivity that he displayed towards her.

Turning over and facing the steps, she heard footsteps climbing up the stairs one at a time.

"Honey, I hope you're hungry...I cooked breakfast for you."

She saw Carter precariously carrying a tray full of homemade pancakes, fried turkey bacon, Texas style fries, grits without sugar, wheat toast, and a large glass of no-pulp orange juice. She was blown away because he was dressed in his nice dark blue suit with his tie swept over his shoulder making sure she had a perfect morning even though that was his day of success.

"Baby, you didn't have to. I know you have to be down at the ceremony at 9 am. I could've gotten a bite to eat when I got up," Audrey said while accepting the tray on her lap.

Carter rushed back down stairs and hurried back up with a tiny black box in hand. He checked his watch and it read 8:11 am.

Smiling nervously, Carter grabbed hold of Audrey's hand on the side of the bed and took a knee. Audrey gasped with turkey bacon in her mouth and covered it with her free hand.

"Baby, I've been thinking about us a lot lately, and since I'm about to become a doctor, I'll have enough money to support us and your shopping habit, I thought that maybe we can get a little closer to the step of marriage, so I got you this..."

Tears streamed down Audrey's face in anticipation as Carter slowly opened the tiny black box. She peered down inside and to her surprise she saw...nothing!

After seeing her reaction, Carter jumped up and laughed. "I said, *about* to be a doctor...girl, you know I ain't got no money right now!"

Audrey laughed and kissed her man before he exited the door. She knew that his heart was pure and when he positioned himself, he would make all of her dreams come true.

"In due time, babygirl, he said walking out of the room.

"I'll be there around 10 baby, to watch you walk across the stage…Love you." Her words echoed throughout the hollowed walls and faintly touched the ears of Carter as he closed the front door.

At noon he walked over to her and introduced himself, "Hello ma'am. My name is Dr. Carter Bradford!" He grabbed her up in his arms and they hugged for what seemed like a lifetime. He pulled out his camera and they leaned in touching faces and he snapped the picture.

They pulled the camera back to take a look. "Perfect!" they said in unison…

Another knock on the door snapped her out of her daydream; Audrey walked back over to the girls in her dressing room and placed the picture back in the album.

Alyssa let their Mom in the room.

"Hey ladies. Honey, aren't you supposed to be getting something done? Your hair or makeup or something?" her mother said immediately feeling the need to control something.

"I'm on time Mom. Everything is on schedule," Audrey said sitting back down at the vanity.

"Well good. I want to be sure that everything runs as smoothly as possible, Audrey. That witch of a planner you have is driving everyone insane. Oh! Here is your grandmother's hair pin," she said handing over the solid gold Swarovski crystal encrusted antique hair pin worn by her grandmother, her mother, and her sister at their weddings.

"The something old," all four ladies said together.

"I'd be honored, Mom," she said taking the pin.

"Well, I'm going to go downstairs and wrangle with that heffa. By the way, the wedding room is beautiful. This is going to be a beautiful day," Mrs. Parchman said making her exit.

The three girls looked at each other and laughed. Mrs. Parchman was never one to back down from a fight but she definitely had one on her hands if she planned on going against Inga!

Something Old...Something New

Chapter 3

The wedding planner, Inga Bergendorf was pacing the floor. Complete with Blackberry, Bluetooth earpiece, checklist attached her clipboard, the epitome of organization, she was.

Audrey's husband-to-be had insisted that she hire nothing but the best to usher in their commitment of a lifetime together. Inga Bergendorf was just that...the best. Wedding planner to the stars is what her professional resume read. She had orchestrated fairy tale weddings for Tinsel town's upper echelon. It was rumored that even Brangelina was on her waiting list.

She stood there in the middle of the huge foyer directing traffic with the sharpness of a Swiss army knife.

There was no room for error in any form or fashion. She was the epitome of perfection right down to the patented leather Fendi pumps she wore.

"Ms. Bur-ger-dwarf, where do you want us to put these flowers?" the young man from the florist inquired.

"First and foremost, let's get one thing straight…it's *Bergendorf!* Can you attempt to say that?" she retorted in a curtsy German accent.

"That's what I said…Burgerdwarf," he said with his shoulders hunched.

"Ber-gen-dorf…say it!" she demanded.

"Ber-gen-dwar…" he hesitated when he noticed the stern look that she was giving him. "Ber-gen-dorf?"

"Thank you," she said rolling her ice blue eyes to the sky that were almost hidden by the black school teacher styled Gucci frames that slid down to the end of her pointed nose. Her jet black hair and porcelain colored skin afforded her plenty of attention from the highest ranks of men but her no nonsense attitude had kept her an unmarried woman for more than 52 years.

But nonetheless, whether single by choice or circumstance, she was a classy woman and had definitely earned her title as best at making other women's dreams come true even if her own dreams seemed too far away to be grasped.

"You can place the flowers there but exercise extreme caution. Those are very delicate flowers. They were flown in from Hawaii this morning," she warned.

"Who the hell is getting married? One of the president's daughters or something?" the young delivery guy asked his partner.

"I don't know but they gotta have some money. I saw the invoice on this delivery and man, they paid $7500 just for these flowers and you know they gotta be paying the Ice Princess a grip," he said motioning back to Inga.

Taking a broad span view of the room Inga was temporarily satisfied that things were running smoothly. There were still five hours before the wedding was set to begin and the decorations were underway, her bride was upstairs in the dressing room and the bridal party was slowly trickling in.

"This may be my best one yet. Lord knows, they deserve the best," she thought to herself. "Then again, that's why they chose me."

She chuckled to herself as her ego couldn't let that one slip by. She turned on her expensive heel and found the next worker to direct.

***

"Come on Jason, I gotta go," Monique whined to her boyfriend. "I cannot be late. Audrey will kill me if that crazy German chick doesn't first."

Monique, who was Audrey's cousin and one of her bridesmaids, pulled the sheet off the bed leaving her boyfriend's naked body exposed.

"We have to be there by noon to get our make-up and stuff done and I know Audrey is probably going crazy right about now," she said turning on the shower in the bathroom.

Jason pulled the comforter off the floor and curled back into the cover. "Well, I'll be there at 2:30. I'm going to get some more sleep." But before Jason closed his eyes and Monique closed the shower doors, he yelled, "You know you could have given me at least five more minutes, you're not in that much of a rush."

With one foot in and the other foot out of the shower, Monique let not only his words but her own personal thoughts sink in. "Maybe he's right. I do have at least five more minutes for the one man in the world that means the most to me…never know what can happen."

Jason felt the comfort of his girlfriend close to his bare skin as Monique let the shower run in her absence.

She snuggled up next to him and kissed him on the lips. She thought about the wedding and how important it was for Audrey. She became emotional as she thought about the love that Audrey and Carter shared. Monique hugged Jason even tighter as tears of joy and pain traced her smooth brown skin.

Thirty minutes later Monique climbed into an ice cold shower for barely five minutes. Enjoying the warmth and comfort from her man, she had totally forgotten the shower was still running.

She was so happy for her cousin. Monique and Audrey were the same age and were the best of cousins. They were thick as thieves when they were young and nothing had changed. They were complete opposites and that's what balanced them out the most.

Monique was a spitfire, she pulled no punches and made decisions at the drop of a dime. Audrey was reserved, conservative, researched and analyzed an entire situation before she made a decision and committed to anything.

That took her back to the week when she couldn't get in touch with Audrey. She was used to talking to her every day and even though she knew that Audrey had started her real estate exam class, that was only two nights out of the week. Monique had called Alyssa and Austin and they both hadn't heard from her either. That was enough for Monique to make an impromptu visit to her cousin's condo.

When she pulled up she was surprised to see a moving truck in front of Audrey's place. She knew this had to be a mistake because Audrey loved her condo and had vowed never to move unless she got married and they all knew the chances of her making a commitment that large was next to impossible. Even more surprising was the fact that the movers weren't taking things out of the house...they were moving things in.

She crossed the lawn, dodging boxes and other pieces of furniture that had been removed from the truck. One of the movers almost tripped over a box as he couldn't take his eyes off of her shapely legs that seemed to run for miles from under the short blue jean skirt she wore.

"Audrey? Audrey, where are you and what is going..." she stopped in mid-sentence as she walked in on a more than friendly kiss between her cousin and who she assumed was one of the movers.

"Mo...hey girl," Audrey said pulling only slightly away from the guy who now faced Monique.

As surprised as she was to see Audrey kissing the man, she couldn't blame her, he was gorgeous.

"Umm...I've been calling you for days. Where the hell have you been?" Monique said walking around the couple taking it all in.

"Well, I've been busy with...him," she said pointing to the guy.

"Okay and, who is...he?"

"Carter, this is my best, best cousin Monique and Monique, this is Carter my...new roommate," Audrey said.

"Okay, we need to talk, now!" Monique said grabbing Audrey by her wrist.

"Nice meeting you, Monique," Carter said as Monique yanked Audrey into the kitchen.

Monique stood in utter shock as Audrey gushed about the new love of her life and how they hadn't separated since the day that they'd met. She couldn't believe that this was her commitment phobic cousin saying that she was moving a complete stranger into her house. This was totally unlike Audrey and it took Monique an hour of listening for her to believe her ears. It was official though, Audrey was hooked!

Monique jumped out of the shower and dried her face and realized that not only were there dots of water from the shower on her face, she was also drying tears.

"I'm so happy for you Audi," Monique said aloud in the steamy bathroom. "You deserve this happiness."

She hurriedly threw on a jogging suit, grabbed her dress, shoes and accessories, kissed Jason and was out the door. Monique was elated to be a part of one of the biggest events that city had seen in a long time.

Chapter 4

"Whoa!" Carter said as he tried to regain control of the 7 series BMW as it fishtailed on Interstate 94. The sudden movement startled Mike awake.

"You okay, man?" Mike asked concerned about his friend.

"Man, it's pretty bad out here," Carter said shaking the uneasiness off.

The snow had really started to come down as they drove directly into the lake effect blizzard. Carter's thoughts immediately rushed back to Audrey. His nerves prompted him to call her but he was almost afraid to take his hands off the wheel. He'd forgotten his Bluetooth device at the house as he hurried out on the kamikaze mission.

He knew she was probably still up. Knowing her she was planning the wedding. That day seemed to consume her. She always said, "The perfect wedding for the perfect couple."

If she wasn't up planning then she was up worrying. He knew she was afraid that something would happen to him. She had expressed that her biggest fear in life was losing the ones she loved. Audrey was protective of her whole family as if she could defy fate or consequence. She took care of them all.

Carter had to admit he had never been with a woman like Audrey. She took care of him. Every night he came home, she fed him and ran his shower. When he got out she was there waiting for him with oil in hand. He was treated to a back and foot massage every night, whether he needed it or not. Audrey was all about satisfying her man, by any means necessary. There wasn't a time that he could remember that he'd gone without love or satisfaction. She truly believed in the "if you aren't doing it, someone else will" saying.

Still in the tumultuous weather, Carter began to second guess his decision and asked Mike about the importance of completing the trip.

"Man, you really think we can make it in all this bad weather, or should we just pull over and wait the storm out?"

Mike, who was all business when it came to business, replied, "Man, we've already driven this far, let's just thug it out. We'll be back home before you know it so you can get back to your girl man, I promise..."

As soon as Mike said those words, the back tires jerked and sent them into a full 360 degree spin out, leaving them on the edge of the shoulder, narrowly missing being struck by a steadily moving Abso-Pure semi-truck.

"Oh shit! Oh shit! You alright, you okay man?!! shouted Mike to Carter as they sat shaken on the side of the road.

Carter answered back slowly, "Ye-yeah, I'm cool. I just can't believe we almost got hit by that truck...damn. I gotta call Audrey," he said dialing her number.

"B-baby..."

Immediately, she knew something was wrong. Carter was never the type to stutter or be at a loss of words.

"What's wrong Carter? Is everything alright?" she exclaimed nervously.

"Baby, you were right. I-I should've waited. We spun off the road..."

"You WHAT?!! Carter, Ohmigod! Baby! Are you okay? Did you crash? Is Mike okay?!!" Audrey knew that she couldn't continue on with her day until Carter made it back home.

"Yeah babygirl, everything's good. We are just going to drive slower, like maybe 10 or 15 miles an hour. It's a blizzard out here. We ran into that lake effect snow. Lake Michigan is only a couple of miles over. But baby, don't worry okay, I'll call you as soon as we reach our destination and are headed back…I love you."

Audrey expressed her love for him and begged him to just pull over and wait the storm out. Carter insisted that he would be okay and that the sooner they took care of business, the sooner he would be back home. Reluctantly, she obliged and hung up the phone.

She thought about calling his mother but decided against it for fear of upsetting her. She told herself that she would wait patiently for his phone call and that everything would be okay. Still, she sat with her stomach upset stirring a cup of morning tea.

Chapter 5

Monique ran past the "Hell Raiser" of a wedding planner that Audrey had hired, hoping that she didn't notice her. No such luck.

"Good morning Monique. So nice of you to join us," Inga sang out as Monique scurried by and rushed up the stairs to the dressing room.

"Good morning," she yelled over her shoulder.

Inga shook her head as the other two bridesmaids, Dana and Crystal ran in together.

"Hey Inga," they said in unison, purposely not stopping to talk to the wedding planner who had given them all hell for 9 months.

"For shame," Inga said to herself with her hands on her hips.

She directed her attention to the last minute details of the wedding.

"Candles...where are the candles?" her voice rang out in the foyer with a 25 foot ceiling. She didn't direct her question to anyone in particular but was more than sure everyone heard her.

***

Dana and Crystal walked into the middle of a hug fest and quickly joined in.

"Hey ladies," Audrey said hugging two of her very best friends. The three girls had been friends since elementary school and were as close as sisters.

"Look at you glowing," Dana said in awe. 'Hmmmm...I hope that's a glow of happiness and not the other glow."

"Hell, let me get married before you start pushing the pregnant thing on me!" Audrey laughed.

"Well, this should get the baby making started tonight," Dana said handing her a La Perla bag.

"Whoooooo!" all the ladies screamed in excitement.

"Hush heffas!" she said snatching the dangling bag. She opened the bag and pulled out the satin and lace garter. She was met with a lot of oh' s and ah's.

"That's your something new!" Dana screamed aloud. Everyone in the room quickly hushed her to silence. They didn't want any reasons to bring the wedding planner from hell up to the dressing room. But it was too late...

Hearing the muffled scream through the brass handled door, Inga swiveled her long neck around and stared in its direction. She contemplated going to see what the commotion was about but retracted the thought.

"That woman has enough on her mind today, maybe I will talk to her a little later..." Inga thought to herself with one hand on her hip and the other pointed to guide a worker in the direction of where the lighting should be.

"Thanks Dana, you're so sweet."

"No problem. Anything for my BFF!"

Seeing all the women that were closest to her all in one room on such a joyous occasion was enough to bring her back to tears.

They had been her support circle for has long as she knew and she definitely needed them that day.

Monique came over and hugged her cousin. She knew that Audrey had to be experiencing a myriad of emotions. Audrey eagerly accepted the comfort.

Finally the bridal party was complete. Shauntel, the matron of honor, Alyssa, the maid of honor and her three bridesmaids Monique, Dana and Crystal.

As if on cue the staff from Jolae Day Spa knocked on the door. The "glam squad" entered with their portable massage tables, makeup bags and hair styling equipment.

The bridal party welcomed them with applause and screams of giddy excitement. The team immediately got down to it. They laid out six portable massage tables which the ladies climbed on and relaxed.

Soon, the tension in Audrey's shoulders was released as the therapist kneaded her back and shoulders. Audrey drifted off to sleep as the other ladies chattered away.

***

"Happy Valentine's Day," Carter sang in her ear, waking Audrey from her slumber.

"Good morning. Happy Valentine's Day baby," she said turning over to face him.

"Unhh unhh!" Carter said covering his nose and pointing to the bathroom. "Hit it, please!"

"Whatever!" she said hitting him on the arm. "Nobody told you to be in my face."

She jumped out of the bed and jumped back as her foot landed on something on the floor. She looked down and saw a chocolate heart covered in red foil. But it wasn't just that one. There was a trail of the candy leading out of the bedroom!

She turned and smiled at him. He sat there with a Cheshire cat grin on his face. His eyes gave her permission to follow the trail.

She slowly followed the path of sweet symbols of love down the stairs and through the hallway. Sun rays crept through the vertical blinds on the patio door creating a heavenly glow to cascade into the room as she followed the last of the hearts leading into the dining room.

She smiled when she saw the room filled with flowers. There had to be six dozen roses around the room. In the center of the table was a small box wrapped in red, pink and white wrapping paper covered in hearts.

Emotions overwhelmed Audrey as she blanketed Carter with an enormous hug. Her hands were shaking with disbelief and joy. She couldn't believe how great of a man she had and was overjoyed at the thought of having him.

With tears in her eyes, "Baby, thank you so much, thank you! I love you Carter, I love you with all of my heart..."

Carter, a bit touched by her reaction, prompted her to open the gift. He leaned against the wall and watched his love exude from the box as Audrey opened it. Her eyes lit up like the stars in the night sky.

"Carter, it's...it's...beautiful." Audrey, still shaking, felt the warmth of his body press against hers as she held the hand-crafted one of a kind ice blue diamond encrusted locket. Inside was the picture of her asleep on his chest.

"Here baby, let me help you put it on..." said Carter in a low tone. Once he clasped the two ends together, Audrey turned and on her tippy toes, reached up and kissed her modern day Romeo. She remembered her heart saying, "I can't wait to marry this man."

"I have another surprise," Carter whispered in her ear as he caressed her back.

"More?" she said taking in the scent of the Irish Spring soap he used.

"Yep, hit the showers Shorty and let's get this day started!"

They ended up at Sweet Georgia Brown's soul food restaurant. Carter gave his name and they were immediately whisked off to a table surprisingly already occupied by an older woman.

Realization immediately set in as Audrey noticed the same flawless caramel complexion and high cheekbones. The woman's dark hair was pulled elegantly back in a bun and was dressed casually in a coral cashmere twin set with tan slacks. The tan Michael Kors sling back high heels didn't go unnoticed by Audrey's keen eye for fashion either.

A sense of anxiety began to settle in the pit of her stomach. She wanted to turn on her heels but Carter had her hand and was pulling her along.

"Surprise!" he mouthed to Audrey as they arrived at the table. He finally released her hand and went around the table to embrace the beautiful woman.

The woman, who was so poised and elegant, waited for Carter to get around the table and grab her hand to help her up.

"Mama," he said hugging her and kissing her on the cheek.

"Carter sweetie, how are you?" she said looking him over. Then she turned to Audrey who was so tense she could do nothing but stand there staring at the two of them. "You must be Audrey. Come here girl and give me a hug. I've heard so much about you that I feel like I already know you."

She held out her arms to Audrey who hugged the older lady and immediately felt a connection.

They talked for an hour even before they ordered brunch. From first glance you would have thought it was Audrey and her mother at the table instead of Carter. The ladies hit it off so well that they decided to meet at least twice a month for a "mother/daughter" brunch. That was the beginning of a beautiful relationship.

As Carter sipped on a glass of sparkling water, he leaned back into the comfortable leather booth and glanced at his perfect view from across the table. He smiled and took a mental picture in his mind of his mother and Audrey hitting it off so well. He felt secure in his heart already about Audrey, but the way that his mother took to her made him even more secure. As the two women chattered, Carter was careful not to let a much wanted tear to drop from his eye. Instead, he held it all in and smiled, again.

***

"Girl, let her rest a while. Today is very important and sensitive for her," whispered the group of girls as they watched Audrey sleeping on the massage table. As she slept softly, the bridesmaid's began to converse amongst themselves their own stories about Audrey and what they knew about Carter.

"Hey, does anyone know if Lance is coming?" Dana asked, glancing at a picture of Audrey, Lance and Carter.

"Oh yeah, Lance..." Crystal said dreamily. All the ladies laughed.

"Yeah, good ole' Lance," Alyssa said remembering the brief time they shared together.

Carter's brother, Corporal Lance Bradford, was nothing less than fine. A career military man, Lance had come home on leave to meet this mystery woman that his younger brother had fallen in love with. Through the letters and phone calls Lance already had love in his heart for Audrey.

Lance knew this woman had to be nothing short of an angel to have captured his brother's heart. It had been a long time since Lance had heard of any 'special' lady in Carter's life. He'd had plenty of women but had steered away from long term relationships and had been that way as long as Lance could remember.

Carter's best friend, Marcus had committed suicide because his girlfriend broke up with him when they were just graduating from high school. The tragedy affected

Carter so badly that he decided he would never love someone that much.

It was mid-April when Lance was finally able to get a two week leave. Their mother had picked him up from the airport and he spent the day with her. They had decided to meet Carter and Audrey for dinner at their house after they hung out and caught up...

"I hope he likes me," said Audrey, rearranging the flowers in the centerpiece of the dining room table. She scurried into the kitchen to stir the Alfredo sauce for the one hundredth time.

"How could he not, girl?" Alyssa asked grabbing the spoon from her sister and turning the sauce off. "What is there not to like about Audi?

"I don't know Alyssa. It's been just those three for so long. I guess I'm just nervous."

"I really think you're over reacting. You need to relax and just go with the flow," Alyssa said rubbing her shoulders. "He's only a man."

Just then the door bell rang. Audrey heard Carter running down the stairs like a kid. He had been upstairs playing the Wii game with the kids and they came running down after him.

Audrey took a deep breath and walked into the foyer to meet the missing piece to the puzzle.

"What's up Big Bro?" Carter said hugging a man that could have been his twin but was two inches taller.

"You got it, lil' Bro. You got it," Lance said as he turned to face the two ladies standing in the entrance way of the living room. "Wow! Who is Audrey, Bro? Either way, you got it made!"

"I know man. They are two beautiful ladies aren't they? But this one has captured my heart," Carter said grabbing Audrey by the hand.

"It's really nice to meet you," Audrey said shaking Lance's hand.

"Girl, get over here and give me a hug," he said almost lifting her off her feet.

Audrey laughed as she instantly warmed to the bear of a man.

"Lance, this is my sister, Alyssa and my niece and nephew, Raquel and Raphael," she said making introductions.

Lance and Alyssa shook hands and were shocked literally by some static cling of some sort.

"Ouch!" Lance said. "You are definitely electrifying!"

"Beauty comes with a price," Alyssa boasted, never the one to be shy.

The group mingled for a while and Audrey served dinner. It was obvious that there was some chemistry between Alyssa and Lance. Carter noticed the secret glances and extra laughs between the two of them. After dinner Alyssa and Lance snuck off to the creek behind the condo.

"I'm really glad I came," Lance said as they walked next to the creek. They stopped as they approached the bridge. Lance, always the gentleman had grabbed her hand and helped her step onto the bridge.

"I'm glad you came, too. I know Audrey is so happy to meet you. She loves your mom," Alyssa said leaning back on the wooden railing.

"Yeah, she's a sweetheart. But I'm even happier because I had the opportunity to meet you," he said moving closer to her.

She was blushing. It's almost if Lance knew she needed the compliments and affection. Newly separated, she was longing for attention and Lance was right on time.

"Well if that's the case, I'm glad you came too."

They were gone for three hours and no one knew what happened and both of their lips have been sealed shut since.

Alyssa blushed as she looked at the picture of her sister, Carter and Lance. The next picture was the trio with an added addition...Lance's wife, Nicole.

After their three hour rendezvous, Lance found it necessary to reveal that he was also married. Though both would have loved to continue this newfound friendship, they both knew it wasn't for the best.

With Alyssa barely out of her marriage and Lance fully engaged in his, there was no room for discussion. What was done was done and from that point forward they were simply, Carter's brother and Audrey's sister.

It was evident that Alyssa carried some hidden feelings for Lance, even after accepting his situation. At family functions she would catch herself wondering what could have been or would catch him staring at her but that one time was and always would be dust under the rug.

Something Old...Something New

Chapter 6

Austin sat on the weight bench in his room after a set of 10 curls with the 45 lb weights. He had a few hours before he had to be at the church for his sister's wedding. He lied back down on the bench and placed his legs in position to work on them. He hated working on his legs, but Carter had pressed upon him that his entire body was the canvas and how would a picture look if only two thirds of the portrait was complete?

He smiled at the thought of him. Carter had entered his life at a very impressionable time. Austin was 16 when Audrey met Carter and it couldn't have been at a better time.

Mrs. Parchman was having a hard time with Austin who had been acting out since he had stepped into the teen years. Her husband had died when Austin was eight and Alyssa and Audrey were already out of the house and in school. Austin had been a "surprise" for the older couple and with no male figure around. Austin was finding a hard time adjusting to the trials of being a teen.

Both Alyssa and Audrey had taken a stab at helping their mother and were at their wits ends. Austin wasn't a bad kid by any means, but when he started high school the attention he was getting became more of a problem than a benefit.

Having played in the Pop Warner football league since he was 6 years old, he had fast become a star in the league and started on his high school team in his freshman year. He was a handsome guy already and the starting football status only encouraged the attention from the girls.

That's exactly where his focus was planted; girls and football. Soon, his grades began to falter and that's when the problems started with his mom. The quiet, studious young man from three years earlier had turned into a force to be reckoned with.

Audrey had brought Carter to Austin's homecoming game where he was being crowned "Duke" in the homecoming court. After the game, in which he threw the winning touchdown, he was surprised to see his sister waiting for him with a guy.

"Hey sweetie," she said hugging her little brother that towered over her by a full foot.

"Hey, wassup?" he said hugging his sister and giving a head nod to the guy.

"Austin, this is my boyfriend Carter. Carter, this is my baby brother, Austin," Audrey said making the introduction.

Carter extended his hand for a handshake and Austin absentmindedly took his hand ready to do the "homeboy" hand shake but Carter firmly held his hand in a bear grip and looked the young man in his eye.

"It's a pleasure to meet you, Austin. I've heard a lot about you," Carter said still holding Austin's hand.

"It's nice to meet you too," Austin said as the cockiness seemed to drain from his body.

There was a wall of respect that was built at that very moment. During conversations thereafter, Austin learned that Carter was a sports fanatic and knew so much about football that he slowly became Austin's personal coach and trainer. They met two or three times a week to work out and Carter was able to make such an impression on Austin that everyone saw the change in the young man and were so grateful.

He recalled the time Carter was cutting his hair and he was bragging about all the girls that were calling his phone. Each time he would get a text message he would show Carter.

"See man...I got this town on lock," Austin bragged.

"I hope you are just as eager to show me that report card when it gets here, man. That's when I'll be impressed," Carter said.

"I'm doing good," Austin responded.

"I want more than good from you Austin. Good is subpar and you are the farthest thing from average. I want excellence from you," he said never stopping the precision cut he was giving Austin.

The only sound in the room was the insistent buzzing of the clippers as the two men thought to themselves.

The lessons that Carter taught Austin extended over to Austin's friends because he wasn't doing the things that he used to do and had explanations as to why when his friends asked what was up.

Carter's theory of 'touch one and teach many' had definitely worked when it came to Austin.

His cell phone rang and brought him back to the reality of today and what it meant for his sister.

"Hey Ma," he answered. "Yeah, I'm getting ready now," he lied getting up from the weight bench.

"I won't be late. I'm fine. Really Ma, I'm okay. I'll see you there in about an hour or so," he assured Mrs. Parchman.

Today Austin was giving his sister away...to the man who she would spend the rest of her life with.

Something Old...Something New

Chapter 7

On an average day, if Carter was watching the big white snowflakes fall into the darkness from the bay window in the living room of the condo, the scene would be beautiful. But driving down Interstate 94 at five o'clock in the morning with the big snowflakes obstructing his view, it wasn't such a beautiful scene. On top of the winds pushing the full sized luxury vehicle around the road like a piece of tumbleweed, this was definitely not a good thing.

Only sleep had stopped Mike's annoying chatter of how he was going to flip the truck that they were going to get and possibly double his investment. Carter was finally able to gather his thoughts and effectively pay attention to the road.

He was still kicking himself for going against his own better judgment and coming down here anyway. He was still shaken from the spinout from earlier. He knew that Audrey was now up and at attention.

"I probably shouldn't have called her," he said to himself. He knew that she was worried now.

His thoughts wandered back to the time when they had broken up. He hated that it had been partially his fault. Never one to leave a situation on bad terms, Carter had always kept in touch with his 'friends' from the past. Even when there were still feelings on the other end, he nurtured the friendship the best he could while still trying to keep distance between the two. One of his old friend's was more persistent than most when it came to expressing her feelings.

He had seen Kim at the Starbucks by the clinic and reconnected. They had been together for a short while but Carter never really felt that connection with her and hated her clinginess so he broke it off as easy as he could, being sure not to hurt her feelings. But Kim wasn't letting go that easy.

They still shared some mutual friends and Kim had heard through the grapevine that Carter had been dating a new girl named Audrey. When Carter sent out his graduation announcement email Kim was able to get Audrey's email address as well.

***

Carter's hands tightened on the steering wheel when he tried to keep control of the car as the wind caused it to sway. They also tightened in anger as he thought back to the bullshit that Kim had pulled.

***

The masseur pushed into the small of Audrey's back as she slept. Her dreams were unpleasant as she was drawn into a nightmare of her run in with Carter's ex-girlfriend, Kim.

It was two days after Carter's graduation and Audrey was showing a house. The young lady had made the appointment a week before and Audrey was supposed to meet with Ms. Jones and her fiancé but he wasn't able to make it.

"This house is perfect for a new family, Ms. Jones. The best part of this home is the backyard," Audrey said as she walked the young lady through the four bedroom suburban home.

"Please call me Kim and yes this house is just right for Carter and I," Kim said looking out the door of the walkout basement.

The words ran past Audrey's ears but she had to have been mistaken. What were the chances that Ms. Jones' fiancé's name would be Carter? Her senses were tingling but she brushed them away. This had to be a coincidence. She gathered her senses and continued the tour of the home.

"So, when is the big day?" Audrey managed to squeak out.

"September 13th. We were waiting for him to graduate from Med school so we could move forward," Kim said. "Now if we can make it to the big day…" she let the sentence linger in the air.

"Your fiancé just graduated from medical school? That's wonderful," Audrey said as her stomach began to rumble.

"Just this past weekend," Kim gushed.

That was all that Audrey could stand.

"Ms. Jones, I-I mean Kim. What is your fiancé last name if you don't mind me asking?"

"No, not at all. His name is Carter Bradford. Do you…uh…know him by chance? Carter is really popular, especially with the ladies," Kim said through a thin smile.

"Umm…no, I don't. I thought…well…he sounded like someone I knew. But…um…I was mistaken. So do think you would be interested in this house at all?" Audrey said recovering from the blow that she had been dealt.

"This house is perfect. We plan on having at least two kids. Well Audrey, let me talk to Carter tonight and I'll give you a call later to let you know what we would like to do. Thanks for showing me the house," she said shaking Audrey's hand.

"Thanks for coming out and I will talk to you soon," Audrey said closing the door. She ran to the half bath off of the kitchen and threw up her breakfast. The same breakfast that Carter Bradford had made for her that morning.

"How could this be? He is with me...all the time. The only time we are apart is when...he is at the hospital," Audrey rationalized with herself.

Then her imagination went into overdrive. Carter had claimed to be putting in doubles for the last two months. There were days when she didn't even see him awake. She had chalked it up to him doing the necessary hours to complete his residency program.

"I can't believe it," she said sinking down into the carpeted living room floor. "I knew it was too good to be true."

Just then her cell phone chimed with a text message. She reached into her bag and pulled out her phone. It was from Carter: Thinking of you. Hope your day is going well. Can't wait to see you later. Love, C.

Her stomach lurched again. She let the phone fall from her hands and stretched out on the floor and cried.

She got another text message a few minutes later: Come meet me for lunch.

She ignored the text and locked up the house. She called Monique to see if she was at work. Monique was a teacher and Audrey wasn't sure if she had taken the summer school spot this year or not.

"Hey girl. What's up?" Monique answered.

"I-I...need to talk," Audrey whispered.

"What's wrong? Where are you?" Monique said pulling her car over.

"I'm just leaving the house in Farmington. I can meet you at the house if you have time," Audrey said as the tears began to fall.

"Of course I have time. I'm on my way," Monique said.

"Thanks Mo," she glanced at her cell phone as it had beeped indicating she had another call coming in. "Wait Mo! Don't hang up, it's him."

She couldn't talk to him yet. No, she needed time to figure this out. She waited until she heard the stutter of beeps indicating that his call had gone to the voicemail before she hung up with Monique.

He called four times before she could make it back to the house. It took everything in her not to answer. She was numb as she pulled up into the driveway behind Monique who had already arrived.

She dragged herself from the car as Monique ran up and grabbed her purse and Messenger bag.

"What happened?" Monique asked.

"I can't believe it. He...is engaged," Audrey whispered as she unlocked the door. Her cell phone was buzzing in her pocket and she knew it was him. This only made her stomach hurt worse.

She slumped onto the chaise lounge in the living room kicking off her sandals. She thought about the beautiful woman who had seemingly destroyed her dreams. Kim Jones wasn't average by any means. Her flawless chocolate colored skin coupled with her long curly hair set her apart from the rest. She was probably 5'9 and her legs were long and defined. Audrey recalled the crisp white dress shirt tucked neatly inside the grey pencil skirt and felt sick again. Everything about Kim seemed perfect and maybe that was why she had Carter.

Monique was in the kitchen getting them some water. Audrey grabbed her cell phone and scrolled down to his messages and missed calls.

Text 1: Hey baby. I know you're busy but I need to know if you are going to meet me for lunch.

Text 2: Is everything ok? Call me as soon as you are done.

Then there were four missed calls. Then Text 3: I don't know what I did but I'm sorry. I need you to answer the phone now.

Audrey set the phone down just as Monique came in and handed her a glass of lemonade.

"I was showing a house today and the lady, Kim said she was engaged to Carter Bradford. Mo, she was looking at the house for her and Carter. My...Carter."

Monique sat there with her mouth hanging open. "This couldn't be," is what she was thinking as she stared at her cousin hoping that she had heard wrong. But from the steady stream of tears that she saw falling from her eyes, she knew she had heard right.

"There's got to be some explanation. Have you talked to him?"

"No, I can't. I can't right now."

"You have to Audrey. You have to at least give him a chance to explain. Everything is not always as it seems," Monique said against her own mind. She wanted to find Carter and kick his ass but she knew the drama wouldn't help her cousin at that point. Besides, Carter did at least deserve the chance to explain himself.

Monique knew how hard this was for Audrey. She'd never given her heart to anyone like she had Carter and for it to all blow up in her face like it seemingly had was devastating.

Audrey's cell phone rang again and she looked at Monique who gave her the nod to go ahead and answer.

"Hello?"

"Baby! What's wrong? I've been calling you. How come you aren't answering?" he screamed into the phone.

"Um...Carter, I met your fiancée today."

He laughed and said, "What are you talking about baby? I didn't get you the ring yet, silly. Now back to why you weren't answering my texts or calls."

"Carter...who is Kim Jones?"

Audrey listened as the pregnant pause consumed the airwaves between the two on either end of the call.

"Um-well, she's an old friend," Carter said shocked by the question.

"Really? An old friend, huh?" Audrey said as the hurt became replaced with anger. "That's funny because I showed her a house today and she said that you two were engaged," Audrey voiced as she stood up and walked to the mantel that was covered with pictures of the couple.

"Bullshit!" he screamed into the phone. "That's a damn lie. Stop playing Audrey, this shit isn't funny!"

"You're damn right it isn't funny! Why would you play games like this Carter? Why did you do this to me?" Audrey screamed into the receiver.

Carter, realizing that it wasn't a joke by the tone in Audrey's voice calmed himself and then responded.

"Baby, this has to be a mistake or something. I don't even talk to Kim. And I damn sure ain't engaged to her. Come on Audi, let's think clearly about this...I'm just as confused as you are."

"This is too much for me Carter. I gotta go!" she said hanging up the phone.

He called right back and she ignored the call. Monique waited for Audrey's reaction because she had heard everything. Something was telling her that there was some shit in the game and it wasn't on Carter's part.

"I can't believe he lied to me like this," Audrey sat back down on the chaise lounge with her face in her hands.

"Audrey, really I think we need to do a little more research into this thing. He said he doesn't even talk to the girl. How did you meet her ass anyway?" Monique asked.

Audrey sat back and thought about her initial contact with Kim Jones.

"I got an email from her about a week ago requesting a list because she was looking for a house," Audrey said.

"Who referred her? Where did she get your information from?" Monique inquired.

Audrey thought back to the phone conversation that they'd had and tried to remember who the woman had said referred her. She was sure that she had asked her because she gave referral fees when an existing client sent someone to her.

"I don't remember…"

***

Carter pressed his foot on the brakes as he noticed the flashing lights of a tow truck a few feet ahead. Another car had slid off the road into the ditch. He tried to focus on the road as his thoughts drifted back to Kim.

***

As soon as Audrey hung up on him he dialed Kim's number.

"Hey Carter. What's up? You changed your mind about us?" she answered.

"Kim, stop playing. What the fuck did you tell Audrey?" he said as quietly as he could as the chief of staff walked past him in the hallway of the emergency room.

"Who is Audrey?" Kim said playing with a stray string on her throw pillow.

"Kim, listen to me. I'm not playing games with you. I've been nothing but nice to you and I need to know what you told my girlfriend," Carter said trying to control his voice as he raced toward the receiving door. He mouthed the word 'lunch' to one of his colleagues and kept it moving to his car.

"Carter, I thought that we should re-visit our relationship. It was too special to just end like that," Kim said in her sexiest voice.

Carter couldn't believe his ears. "Look Kim. I'm not trying to hurt your feelings but what we had wasn't special at all. We've been over for a long time and this bullshit you just pulled might have cost me something that is very special to me. You better hope like hell that I can fix this," he said hanging up the phone.

He sped down the streets barely stopping at red lights. He knew that she was probably at home. He also wasn't surprised to see Monique's car there in the driveway as well. That was Audrey's better half.

He was a bundle of nerves as he turned the key into the door. The first person he saw was Monique. She was standing in front of Audrey who looked like she had just lost her best friend. His heart strings pulled at the sight of the tears on her face.

"Audrey, listen to me. It's all a big misunderstanding. Please believe me," he said walking to her. Monique surprisingly moved aside so he could get to Audrey who instinctively turned away from him.

He reached for her arm and she pushed his hand away. She wasn't saying anything as he pleaded with her to just listen. She snatched away from him as he tried to hug her from behind.

"I'm going over Monique's, Carter. I don't want to see your face right now," was all she said as she grabbed her purse and walked out the door.

***

Audrey ruffled in her sleep as the dream climaxed in her slumber causing her muscles to contract even more. The masseur shook his head as he knew she had to be stressed out. This was a colossal day for her. He continued kneading the muscles as best he could as she continued to rest…

That night at Monique's house she went back over every piece of correspondence that she had from Kim Jones. She went into her email account and did a search on the name, Kim Jones and was surprised when Carter's graduation email popped up as well. She scanned the email addresses that he had sent the announcement to and sure enough Ms. Kim Jones was one of the recipients.

Audrey shut the computer down and checked her voicemails. She had 10 total; all from Carter. The last one made all the pieces to the puzzle fit.

"Baby, I am so sorry that this is happening but it's not what you think. This dumb ass girl set you up. I don't talk to her at all. The last time we communicated was when I sent the graduation email out and she replied to the email just saying congratulations. I swear to God that it's nothing more than that. I love you. Please don't act in haste. Please answer the phone. I know it's hard but we need to talk. I would never do anything to hurt you Audrey. You mean everything to me. Please just give us a chance. I'll be up if you want to call me tonight. I'm working a double. I'm waiting on you, baby."

The realization that she had been duped hit her like a ton of bricks.

"That bitch!" Audrey said aloud.

She sat back on the headboard of the bed in Monique's guest bedroom. Monique walked in to check on her and Audrey ran the whole story down to her.

"So she got your email address from the email he sent out and contacted you. This bitch is really out of her mind, huh? But you know we got something for that, right?" Monique said cracking her knuckles.

"Yeah, you know that's right. I feel so damn stupid. How could I let her ass trick me like that? I know Carter and I trust him. I don't know why I didn't give him a chance to explain. No woman can ever tell me anything about him," she said throwing her laptop into her bag.

"I take it we aren't having a sleep over now," Monique said lying on the bed.

"I'm going to get my man, girl," Audrey said hugging Monique and running to her car.

It was 11pm and she knew the hospital staff was in the middle of shift change but she had to talk to him. She ran into the emergency room and smiled at Otis the Security guard as he buzzed her into the back.

"I hope you are going back there with some good news because that boy has been walking around like he lost his puppy," the old man said to Audrey as she walked through the heavy double doors.

She was surrounded by sickness and a million people in green scrubs but none of that dissuaded her from finding him. She saw him standing at the nurse's station looking over a chart and ran over to him.

She wrapped her arms around his waist and hugged him from behind. He turned around and grabbed her up in his arms.

"Baby..."

"No, let me first," she said interrupting him. "I'm so sorry for doubting you. I know you would never, ever hurt me and I am so sorry for letting someone come between us. I love you so much Carter," she said with tears in her eyes.

"It's okay, baby. I'm sorry for letting her get to you. I should have protected you better. You mean everything to me," he said staring deeply into her tear-filled eyes.

"I didn't know what to think, but I should have known better."

"Kim is a damn psycho. I don't doubt that she was pretty convincing. We'll deal with that later but right now I need you to know that I would never hurt you. I know that we will have some bad days, but trust and believe they will be kept to a minimum if I have anything to do with it and they damn sure won't have anything to do with another woman," Carter said rubbing her back as he held her close.

Audrey felt his soul intertwined with hers at that very moment. She was so happy that she didn't lose such a wonderful man. As he held her tight, she thanked the Lord for the day they had met.

***

"Ok, Audrey," the masseur said waking her from her slumber. "Time to get up, sleepy head."

"I love you," Audrey said as she pulled herself from her dream.

Tony, the masseur replied with a smile, "Well damn, I know I'm good but I didn't think I made you fall in love with me!"

The other ladies laughed as a slightly embarrassed Audrey sat up blushing.

Something Old...Something New

Chapter 8

"That was a close call," Carter thought to himself. "I could have lost the woman of my dreams, on the account of some bullshit."

His thoughts were interrupted by Mike's snoring and the ache in his knees from riding so long.

"Chicago 73 miles," he read aloud as he nudged Mike who sleepily rose up.

"Wassup? You straight man? Damn, I must have fallen asleep," he said through a yawn as he stretched and looked out the window.

"I'm straight but I think we should pull up though. I need to stretch my legs," Carter said sitting straight up to stretch his back.

"Damn Cee, I know you like, how this brotha falling asleep while I'm driving and this is his mission, huh?" Mike laughed.

"Naw Bro, you know you straight. I just need to stretch a little and we'll be good to go. Damn! I just missed the exit ramp. I can barely see. We can come up at the next exit to get some gas."

"Man, I really appreciate you coming out with me. You know these opportunities come and go so quick, and I couldn't pass this one up. I know you wanted to get in bed with lil' mama," Mike said.

"You know she was tripping, right?" he said smiling at his friend.

"I knew she would be. She's going to kick my ass when we get back. You're lucky though man. She loves you so much," Mike said.

"I know. You know I've had my fair share of women…"

Mike interrupted him, "Man, you had enough for the both of us!"

They laughed as Carter continued, "I know but for real man, not one of them can compare to her. I think I had so many women because I would get one quality from one but then she would be missing another. So I looked for that quality in the next woman, but with Audrey, it's different. No woman can stand next to her pound for pound, even if she is only a buck twenty soaking wet! She handles me and keeps me in check, with her short ass!" he said laughing.

Mike agreed that she was definitely the one for him. "That's good bro. That's real good to see you happy, man. Anybody that can get you to focus on them for more than a month is definitely the right woman for you...with your 'bros before h-...'

Carter cut him off before he could finish that statement. "Alright, watch it now. My woman is my princess and my queen."

Mike playfully punched him in the shoulder and commented, "I know bro, I know. Audrey is a good woman. She deserves to be a wife, man. Women like that don't last long on the market, bro. You made the right decision with that, forreal."

"Yeah man, I remember that special moment that I made her mine," said Carter as he drifted down memory lane...

"Baby, where you at?" questioned Carter as he rushed into their home jogging up the steps. As he entered their bedroom, he saw a lump in the comforter indicative to where Audrey was sleeping. Excitedly, he whisked over to her and gently shook her.

"Wake up sleepy head...wake up!" whispered Carter in Audrey's left ear. Groggily, she pulled the comforter back over her head and mumbled something barely audible.

"Sleepy...too early Carter, wake me up in an hour."

Carter, smiling as he walked to the foot of their pine oak sleigh bed, dug his hands beneath the comforter and tickled her size 5 and a half feet.

She immediately jerked her feet upwards toward her torso and screamed, "Leave me alone Carter! I'm sleepy! We didn't go to bed until four last night...why are you up anyways? Come back and lay down, or go downstairs. Whatever you do, just let me sleep." She readjusted the plaid comforter yet again and whined, "Go away...see you later boyyy! Dang, you play too much!!!"

All of a sudden, a horn from an unfamiliar car sounded off. Carter peered out of the window as Audrey turned to face the other side of the dimly lit room with a pillow over her face. Carter smirked sneakily as he rushed back to Audrey's side.

"Come on baby, for real...you have to get up. I know you're still sleepy from last night but today's your

BIRTHDAY! I have a surprise for you, baby!" He kissed her on the forehead and nudged her out of the bed.

Audrey, now sitting up slowly, looked around as her eyes started to focus. She stood up and grabbed her robe as she slipped her feet into her bunny rabbit eared house shoes. As she passed him, she pushed him aside in frolic and walked down stairs to wash her face and brush her teeth. She was happy on the inside because she loved surprises, especially from her baby.

As soon as the bathroom door shut, Carter ran down the carpeted steps and zoomed back outside. In less than a minute, he was inside again awaiting Audrey's exit from the bathroom.

"What is it Carter, what's my surprise...and it better be good!" She said dauntingly.

That was the moment he had been waiting for. Carter stood up from the sofa and ushered for her to come close. As she obliged, he swiveled around her and placed both hands over her eyes as he guided her to the window.

Her heart was racing. She could feel his heartbeat on the back of her neck. She could hear his breathing increase with excitement as they approached the window. "What is it?" she thought happily. "What has this boy done now? Is it a new car? Naw, we don't have enough money for that yet…dangit. He better hurry up and show me, whatever it is!"

Finally, the two were in front of the living room window. Carter slowly removed his hands and opened the blinds. Before anything else entered the room, the sunlight barged its way in. Audrey squinted and turned her head slightly. It was 72 degrees at eleven o'clock in the morning on that bright and sunny day in April. As her eyes made the last adjustments, a black on black 550 Benz limousine awaited her outside.

"Carter, what's going on baby?!!" she asked excitedly.

Humbly, he replied, "You. I want this day to be a day you never forget. Now go on inside and enjoy yourself. Lean back and relax, sip on a little bit of that bubbly and enjoy the ride."

"But where am I going? And look at me, I'm a mess! I didn't do my hair, my nails aren't even touched up." Gesturing to her boy shorts and tank top, she continued to rant. "I mean for real? Where am I going to go with this on? Be serious, I'm half naked!"

"I see, that's why I'm giving you all of 10 minutes to through on something and hit it, okay? Trust me sweetheart, it will be well worth it…"

She turned and stood on her tiptoes to kiss him. "But baby wait, you're not going with me?"

He knelt down and with both hands around her waist, kissed her back. "No baby, this day is all yours...I'll be waiting in the wings, okay? Now stop stalling and pull some jeans up on that ass!"

He handed her a love tap on her dairie aire as she rushed upstairs. Down faster than he could blink, Audrey kissed him goodbye and headed out the door to the awaiting limo.

***

Audrey was in shock as the sweet smell of freshly cut roses surrounded her as she stepped inside. Roses were decorated throughout the limousine. As she looked at the pattern and color sequencing of flowers, she saw her named spelled out! That was too much for her as she took it all in. Champagne was already sitting on ice with a beautifully designed box on the seat with a note attached. The driver rolled down the partition window and told her his instructions.

"Ms. Parchman, we will be taking the scenic route today, if you don't mind."

Caught up in the moment, all she could do was nod. As they pulled off, she received a text from Carter that read,

"Hey, there is a list of destinations for you today. Open up the card alongside the armrest. The rest is inside."

Frantically, Audrey searched for the armrest and lifted it up. Finding the note, she opened it and it read, "Are you SURPRISED YET?!!!" It had a picture of Carter in the middle of the card.

Audrey smiled as she cried from excitement. She continued to read the card. "Today is your day sweetheart, the driver will be taking you to a couple of places so sit back and relax." P.S. Don't open up the box either until instructed to...Don't' ruin the surprise, Shorty!"

Audrey just couldn't believe it. That was so sweet of him. How could she have met a man so perfect for her...so right? She thanked GOD for sending him as she reclined in the ash grey seats and rocked herself back and forth to the sweet melodies of one of her favorite jams by Amil Larieux, For Real.

***

Carter ate breakfast alone as he twisted a 3 carat round solitaire platinum engagement ring around the tip of his right thumb. He had about twenty more minutes before Audrey and the driver reached their next destination.

***

The driver headed downtown just as the stores began to open. He parked then walked around to Audrey's door where he opened it and helped her out. The sun was beaming and Audrey frowned because she had forgotten to grab her sunglasses.

As the two of them walked towards the entrance of the Gucci store, the driver rushed in front and met her at the door as he held it open.

All Audrey could do was text her sister and best friend the play by play events that were going down. She looked at the price of a pair of black Gucci style sandals and quickly sat them down. A very petite female sales associate walked over and asked Audrey for her name.

My name is Audrey Parchman, why do you ask?"

The associate replied, "Great, we were expecting you. Did you want to try on those?"

The associate pointed to the eleven hundred dollar pair of sandals that Audrey had just snatched her hands away from.

"Stuttering, she replied, "Uh, no thank you. They are a little bit steep for my price range."

The associate leaned in and whispered, "Today we were informed that you don't have a price range." And with a smile, she whisked off to the back to get the pair of shoes; in all the colors available.

***

"Hey, is everything set down there?" asked Carter sitting in front of the blank television screen that was mounted to their living room wall.

"Yes Carter, everything is set and in place. Guests should be arriving at the Pontchartrain around 6:30, right?"

"Perfect, that's perfect Alyssa. Make sure everyone is in place for the surprise. This is a birthday she'll never forget."

***

The driver of the limousine tucked away the purchases and helped Audrey out of the heat and back into the cool insides of her temporary paradise. Two pair of Gucci heels and a hand bag later totaling $3,900 dollars, Audrey was in a state of euphoria. She didn't care where she went next; as far as she was concerned, shopping was the highlight of her day.

They coasted off of the waterline and went into the suburbs of Detroit. The limousine pulled up and parked in front of a ritzy dress shop. All of the celebrities came there when they needed a dress that would speak volumes, and now Audrey found herself in front of the classy boutique.

"Ohmigod!!! The Vert Nouveau?!!! Are we, are we really going here? Ohmigod! I love that man so much!!!" Audrey said through trembling lips and tears being wiped away from her eyes. The driver handed her an envelope and instructed her to give it to the associate inside before she did anything else.

Once inside, Audrey spotted the owner and dress maker behind the beaded door and handed him the envelope. As he unsealed it and read the note, he gave Audrey a once over. She, in turn gave him one back. Her body language shouted, "What?"

"Well, birthday girl, someone must really love you! Follow me," the owner suggested. His over accentuation of the letters S and T made Audrey giggle to herself.

Once the two made it to the back of the store, he pulled out five beautifully made by hand, one of a kind dresses. Audrey was floored at all of the attention given to her.

"Take your time my dear. There is no rush, I guarantee you. Time is on your side today…" He offered her his personal dressing room and went back up front to attend to the other customers. Five minutes later he returned to have his breath taken away.

"You look ab-ssolutely amaz-zing! You are a goddess, princess! That's the dress for you!"

Audrey looked in the mirror and saw an angel staring back at her. The dress she had on seemed to have been made just for her. Besides the usual snipping and hemming, it fit perfectly. The soft blue and teal Vera Wang dress clung to her body, giving off a sensuous feel of sexiness. The off the shoulders and invisible line tie that teetered all the way down to the small of her back shouted Womanhood. The off center split that ran alongside the inseam of her left thigh gave it that expensive 'you only wear this once look.' Indeed, she was all set and ready to go with that one.

"I think, I think I'll take this one," she said.

The owner screamed back, "I just bet you would honey child! Give me about twenty minutes to touch it up and you will be all set, okay?" Audrey nodded and headed back to the dressing room to change. Twenty two minutes later, the owner met her at the door and handed her the dress.

"How, I mean, well, is it free?" asked Audrey a bit confused.

"Listen baby, as you keep moving in your life you will learn that nothing in life is free…not even love. Love comes with a price; a price that feels good or one that feels bad. Nevertheless, it costs girl! And so does this dress! Hell naw it ain't free! Your beau handled it. Like I said, you are all set sweetie...take care, toodles!" He blew her a kiss as she headed to the car where the driver stood waiting with the door open. He took the dress and carefully placed it inside of the limousine's storage compartment.

She was exhausted and honestly ready to go home. Audrey asked if they were done for the day and the driver slowly shook his head no. "We have a couple of more stops and we should be done, okay?"

***

Carter called his brother to make sure he was still able to show up, if only for a minute. After that conversation, he checked his watch and wondered if Audrey and the driver were on schedule. It was 2:35 pm and they should be at either the nail place or the massage parlor. He decided to take a nap until five. Carter set his alarm and decided to get ready then.

***

The driver of the limousine let Audrey out and walked her up to the double doors of 'Serenity Place', an upper echelon day spa. Again, the driver reached inside of his pocket and retrieved a white envelope that he handed to

Audrey. Glancing at his watch, he informed Audrey that he would be back in two hours, giving her time to enjoy herself.

A beautiful young lady greeted Audrey and asked for her name. A reservation was intact and as she looked over the services booked for her, the greeter had to step back and gasp.

"Wow, I see you're getting the works, and you are right on time for your appointment. Let me show you to our shower room where you can cleanse your skin and allow our alkaline waters to purify your pores."

Audrey stepped out of her jeans and pulled off her top. She stuffed her belongings inside of a personal locker and stepped into the already running, six head, four angled shower. Instantly, she began to feel the power of the water working through her skin. She would have stayed in there forever if she could. There was a knock on the door that startled her back into reality.

"I must have been taking too long," she mumbled to herself as she quickly dried off with one towel and wrapped another over her frame. "I'm ready," she lied.

In two and a half hours, Audrey's body was pulled, pushed, heated, cooled, pressed on firmly, caressed on gently, karate chopped, and stretched into a myriad state of relaxation. She had never felt so good before in her entire life. From the warm stones placed on her back for tension release to the lettuce body wrap to deduce body fat, Audrey was completely satisfied. In the interim, she also received a facial, manicure, and pedicure. She couldn't wait to see Carter so she could tell him how much she loved him and how much he meant to her.

All the girls in the spa whispered to each other, wondering who Audrey was as she walked out with her personal driver awaiting her at the door. At last, home sweet home she thought. But the day was not over yet.

***

Carter's alarm had sounded a half an hour ago. He slept over and when he finally awoke, he had to rush to get ready. He pulled out his black three piece suit and a crisp white Italian style dress shirt with winged tips. Carter reached underneath the bed and retrieved a box that contained a black pair of alligator skin shoes. "Yeah, I haven't worn these since, since...my best friend's funeral," he thought to himself as he wiped them off, removing the stubborn grass that chose to stay underneath the heel. Dressing quickly, Carter sent out a courtesy text to Alyssa assuring her that everything was going as planned.

***

Elated at the day's events, Audrey leaned back and plucked the petals from her roses. She looked listlessly out of the tinted windows and found a new appreciation for living. Chicago's skyline was electrified by the tall buildings with the pristine blue waters behind them. She felt so much love that she never wanted that day to end. Audrey recognized at that very moment that she and Carter were meant to be together; that they were in fact, soul mates.

"Ms. Parchman, this will be our last stop, I assure you," said the driver as the partitioned window lowered halfway.

Audrey smiled at the driver in appreciation. At that very moment, sitting in that very limousine, Audrey felt that life was at its best. She felt that nothing at that particular moment could convince her to believe or feel otherwise.

The driver double parked and helped her out of the car. He carried her bags to the bell hop and thanked her for her time. She was overwhelmed at his excellent service. Audrey offered a tip but he emphatically refused.

"I have been taken care of already, Ms. Parchman. But thank you anyways. Here is the last envelope of the night. Enjoy."

Just as he began to close the limousine's passenger door, he shouted for her to wait.

"Ms. Parchman, you are forgetting something. I do believe this is for you." He handed her the box that was in the limousine from the beginning.

"Oh, thank you so much. You're absolutely right!" Audrey grabbed the 12 by 16 inch box and headed for the front desk. The clerk looked up her name and saw that the Presidential Suite had been reserved several months ago for this day.

"You are all set Ms. Parchman. The room number is 1211. Oh, and there's a note attached for you inside."

Audrey thanked her and followed the bell hop to the elevator. He kept staring at her.

"You must be some type of celebrity's wife, but I don't see a ring," he said in his Jamaican accent.

Blushing, Audrey said to the bell hop, "Well, he's a celebrity in my heart and the ring, well we're working on that. Marriage is forever, you know. It's a big step."

The brass elevator doors sprang open and the two of them stepped on. The bell hop continued the conversation.

"Yes, it is. And that is the beauty of it; forever. That means that out of this whole wide world, you found somebody to love and be with forever, no matter what happens. Why are you waiting so long? Do you really love him? Do you really think he is the one?"

The conversation couldn't keep up with the quick elevator ride. As the doors parted, the bell hop took the lead and led her down a long corridor.

"Yes, I do love him and I know he is the one. I just think that everything has its own time and place, that's all. Marriage is in the works, but not exactly at this moment." She felt the whole commitment phobia coming to life as they walked down the hallway.

Never turning around, the bell hop shouted behind him, "Well, when is the time? You ever heard of that saying, here today, gone tomorrow? That's real, I can assure you. My wife died of cancer just before our 13th anniversary. There's nothing I wouldn't do to have her back again."

Audrey felt so bad for him. Her heart ached for the man. Something changed in her heart at that moment. She couldn't imagine a day without Carter in her life. He truly meant the world to her and she felt that he was the other half to her whole being.

"I'm so sorry to hear that," she said.

The bell hop opened the door to her suite and sat her bags down in the foyer. "Live everyday as if it was your last, little lady," he said as he quietly exited the room.

Minutes later Audrey jumped on the oversized king bed fit for a queen and opened up the last note. Carter had reservations for two at the top of the hotel at an upscale five star restaurant. Even though her birthday was full, she didn't fret. She needed to be downstairs by eight o'clock and it was already after seven. She finally opened the box and tears streamed down her rosy red cheeks.

There was the black ring box that he had tricked her with before with yet another note. It instructed her to go to the closet where she would find the shoes and stockings to match her dress. Also, the note instructed her to open up the chest where she would find an elegant bra and panty set by Victoria Secrets Exclusive Collection....

"Man, you ain't do all that!" shouted Mike from the passenger's seat.

"Dude, let me tell the story man, dang! And I did all of that and some that night," Carter fired back with an added amount of testosterone.

"How you pay for all that then?" challenged an incredulous Mike.

"Now you all in my pockets! You forgot, huh? Remember, I had just started at the clinic and they gave me a hefty bonus and I had been working double shifts for months. I spent every red cent on my baby that day, but my baby's worth it. Now let me get back to the story, I'm almost to the good part..."

Audrey sat alone at the table after checking in for her reservation. She glanced at her watch and readjusted it on her left wrist. She sipped on some water and waited for Carter.

***

Carter was inside of the conference room with Audrey's mom and siblings. They were in the front and back of him with Carter in the middle as their hands were clasped around him. They surrounded him in prayer for what he requested of them. After the prayer, Carter hugged everyone and rushed out to the next room. Inside he found his mother, his brother and Lance's wife. They too laid hands on him and put prayer around their loved one. The presence of the Lord was in the room. He kissed his mother and hugged his brother as he ran out of that room to meet Audrey.

As soon as she saw him striding inside, her heart rate increased. She stood, awaiting the man of her dreams to thank him for spoiling her as he had. He spotted her with the help of the server and quickly wasted no time.

Their eyes were locked. Carter was as handsome as he could be in his suit and Audrey was as beautiful as the feathers on the wings of angels. His mind was racing. Her thoughts were chasing her emotions. She would definitely remember her 28th birthday, thanks to Carter.

"You look impeccable," Audrey managed to say as Carter pulled up a chair.

"Thank you baby, you look so fine right now..." he replied.

As she sat across from him, the two just stared at each other. She thanked him over and over again in her mind for her birthday, but knowing Carter, she had a funny feeling that something more was in place.

"Baby, I love you and I hope that this day, the very day that GOD sent you down from heaven is a day that you will always cherish. I'm not too big on words but it's something that's been on my mind for a while now."

Audrey took a deep breath as the lighting dimmed. Her family walked in along side of his. She couldn't contain the tears anymore. She knew what was about to happen.

"Baby, before I ask you to marry me, there are some people in front of you that I have to ask something of."

Carter pushed back his chair and kneeled down in front of Audrey's mother.

"Mrs. Parchman, I love your daughter with all of my heart. I need your permission. I need your blessings. I need the love and support of your family if I have a chance at having a successful marriage. I commend you for raising your children and for running your household the way that you did and I love you for molding Audrey into the woman that she is today. Mrs. Parchman, I'm asking from you, Audrey's hand in marriage.

Mrs. Parchman wiped the tears from her eyes and took his hand in her own. "Carter I couldn't ask for a better son-in-law. Of course you have my love, my support and my blessings." She kissed his cheek and turned him to face her youngest daughter.

The other guests were overwhelmed by what was happening. Audrey was shaking with tears as Alyssa stood by her side until Carter turned and knelt in front of her.

"Baby, there you have it..." Carter teased with a smile. "No but for real, I don't want to keep you waiting all day. You know that I love you more than anything and that I'll do anything for you. I will never leave you, never forsake you, never stop loving you baby, never...will you marry me?"

Chapter 9

"Alright! Enough teasing me!" Audrey said sitting up on the massage table. "Okay, what's next?"

Dionne the makeup artist chimed, "That would be me."

"Great! Let me go wash my face again," Audrey exclaimed hopping off the table.

Crystal was getting her brown sugar foot scrub and looking through the photo album. She laughed when she saw a picture of Audrey and Carter at the Renaissance Festival with a real life 'knight in shining armor'.

"They are the cutest couple," she thought to herself as she enjoyed her foot massage and pedicure. She leaned her head back and closed her eyes. She recalled one of the worst nights of her life. She had been out on a date with a guy named Darius. When they finished dinner he suggested they go to a party that one of his frat brothers was throwing.

She'd already had two glasses of wine at the restaurant and was feeling a little tipsy. But tipsy was never good enough for Crystal. She was an all around party girl and she drank to get drunk. When they got to the party, Darius headed straight for the bar with Crystal in tow.

Darius and his friends started ordering shots and she was hanging right with them. After three shots of Patron, she needed to hit the restroom. She was feeling really weird. Not just tipsy, it was like she couldn't focus and was feeling really dizzy. On her way there she bumped into a guy walking out of the bathroom. It happened to be Carter.

"Hey Crystal, what are you doing here? Whoa! You alright?" he asked as she stumbled into him.

"Umm…hey Carter. No…umm…I'm not feeling too hot," she slurred as she clung to the wall.

He turned her to face him and looked at her face. She was sweating up a storm, so he guided her into the bathroom and sat her down on the edge of the tub.

He wet some paper towel and wiped her face. As he lifted her eyelids to check the dilation of her pupils he immediately knew that she was high off of some type of drug.

"Crystal, have you taken any type of pills or some other type of drug?" he asked sternly but she was no good. She was slumping down and could barely hold her head up. Then she bent over and vomited into the toilet. He could only estimate what her body temperature was but he knew it was elevated. All the classic signs of an ecstasy overdose.

Just as he had placed her in the shower and turned on the cold water, Darius came into the bathroom.

"Wassup man? I know you not trying to get a piece of the action. I just got her primed up and ready to go," Darius chuckled while leaning back on the door.

"What the fuck did you give her?" Carter snapped, getting in Darius' face.

"What the fuck is your problem, Cee? I gave her a little X. She was ready for it anyway. I just helped her along. Did you see how this tramp drinks?"

Before he knew it Carter had punched him in the mouth and was pounding on him with all his strength until one of the frats pulled him off of Darius.

Darius laid there curled up in the fetal position as everyone gathered around the two. The guy that was holding Carter could barely restrain him and was looking around for some help.

"Let me go," he demanded as he snatched away and walked back into the bathroom. Crystal was still out of it so he picked her up and took her to his car.

Audrey had been out with Monique and Dana and was just getting in when Carter pulled up. She watched as he went around to the passenger side and pulled Crystal out and carried her up to the porch.

"What happened? Carter what happened?" she asked frantically opening the door.

Carter took Crystal straight to the bathroom and put her back under the cold water. He explained the situation to Audrey and they both sat there until Crystal's body temperature was regulated and she started to come around.

When she finally opened her eyes and saw Carter and Audrey sitting there looking worried, all she could do was cry. They promised to keep that incident to themselves.

"Please don't judge me," she cried.

"We won't judge you. We're going to help you," Carter said.

The next day Crystal started her AA classes and had been sober for 547 days. She was so grateful to the both of them because they had been there every step of the way.

She closed the book just as the lady finished her brown sugar foot scrub. She hid her face in the towel so no one would see the tears that fell from her eyes. She owed them both so much and was so happy to be there to support her best friend as she had supported her.

Chapter 10

Dana walked over to where Crystal was getting her pedicure and noticed her cleaning her face. "Hey, are you alright?"

"Who? Oh yeah, I'm straight. The fragrant salt in the water was getting to my eyes," she said wiping her face clean of the tears that she had shed.

"Ooo! Let me see the album. Everyone is talking about the pictures that Carter took for Audrey. I've got to see them," Dana said grabbing the album and having a seat on the chaise lounge.

She flipped through the first two years of Audrey and Carter's relationship. She stopped at a black and white of Carter obviously just getting out of the shower with a white towel wrapped around his waist. The sight of Carter's nearly naked body gave her pause and she quickly flipped the page. This time she was greeted by a picture of him asleep that Audrey must have taken.

Old memories came tumbling back. No one ever really knew that she had harbored a secret crush on Carter from the first time she met him, except him...

They were at Alyssa's housewarming party and Carter had been in the kitchen straightening up when Dana came in the kitchen to refill the spinach dip bowl.

"Hey, uhhh Dana, right?"

"Yep that's me. How are you Carter?" she said quickly taking notice of his toned shoulders, arms and chest through his fitted t-shirt. He was rocking the white boy look with a v-neck white tee, some True Religion jeans and some navy Chuck Taylors. He literally topped it off with a Detroit Tigers fitted cap with the old English 'D' emblazoned on the front.

"I'm good, just doing my part. I'm mad that nobody brought their boyfriends with them. Why am I always the only guy?" he asked leaning up against the sink.

Dana couldn't help but notice that even when he wasn't modeling, he looked like a model.

"Because you're the only one who doesn't mind being surrounded by all of us cackling hens," she laughed. "If I had a man I would make him come, too."

"Well, we're going to have to work on that so I can have some more testosterone at these things," he said leaning over to wipe the side of the spinach bowl with the dishrag. She couldn't help but to smell the old school Issey Miyaki cologne he was wearing.

"Thanks," she said picking up the bowl and turning to join the other ladies in the living room. It was at that very moment that she realized a crush had formed on her behalf for her best friend's man.

Though, never in a million years would she act on it, it was undeniable that she had feelings. Even when he came and joined Audrey on the couch, Dana couldn't help staring at him.

She would never intentionally do anything to hurt Audrey, who had been the best friend that anyone could ever have. That's what made it easier for her to contain the lustful feelings that she was harboring for Carter. If it had been anyone else other than Audrey, she would have had to at least see where his mind was at.

One day she and Audrey were going to hang out and Dana had arrived at their house before Audrey got finished at the hairdresser. She sat in the driveway checking her emails from her phone when she saw a pair of headlights pull up behind her. She assumed it was Audrey and got out of the car.

Carter came walking up the driveway, "Hey Dana. Audrey should be here in about 20 minutes." He motioned for her to follow and continued, "You can wait inside if you want," he said while unlocking the side door of the condo without waiting for her answer.

She immediately noticed his slender frame in the scrubs that he was wearing that hung low on his hip bones. He had on an undershirt that clung to his muscular chest and his arms were magnificent. She watched as he thumbed through the mail then threw it on the counter.

He looked back absently at her and said, "You don't have to wait in here. You can wait in the living room. Audi should be here in a few minutes. If you'll excuse me, I gotta go take this crap off," he yelled over his shoulder as he headed towards the stairs.

Dana sat down at the breakfast bar and grabbed the Ebony Magazine that he had thrown on the counter and flipped through it. Her heart jumped when she heard him start the shower. Though she was able to control her feelings for him the thought of seeing him in the shower got the best of her.

She knew the layout of Audrey's condo and was sure that you could see directly into the master bathroom from their bedroom door. Dana also knew that the shower door was all glass, an added bonus for her secret master plan. She went back and forth with her conscience for a minute before the 'little devil' on her shoulder won the argument.

She crept up the stairs and tiptoed down the carpeted hallway. She heard the shower still running and her mouth was watering with the anticipation of finally seeing the body that she secretly lusted over.

She peeked her head in the door with her fingers crossed that he had not closed the bathroom door either.

"Bingo," she said to herself.

Then she was startled by someone clearing their throat behind her. When she turned around she was face to face with Carter who was holding fresh linens and a towel in his hands.

"I was just...I was looking for..." she stammered.

"The bathroom..." he finished her sentence with his knowing eyes burning into her own shameful ones.

"I'm really sorry, Carter," she said looking down at her feet.

"It's cool. You can wait for Audrey...downstairs," he said pointing down the hall to the stairway.

She was so ashamed that she made up an excuse to Audrey that she wasn't feeling well and they didn't go out that night.

She waited for weeks for a sign that Carter had told Audrey what she had done but none ever came. Audrey was still the wonderful friend that she had always been and Carter kept his distance but was always cordial.

"I guess the guilt was punishment enough he figured," Dana thought to herself as she closed the album.

Dana was so grateful to him. He could have easily told Audrey what Dana had done and they wouldn't be friends today. She regretted making such a dumb decision and would never risk her friendship again. The experience made her a better person and she thanked Carter for that.

Dana went and stood in line for her makeup and prepared to stand up for her best friend in the whole wide world.

Chapter 11

The room was filled with excitement as the time was drawing near. Audrey had just sat down to get her makeup done. Dionne was focused on applying the makeup so they weren't talking. This gave her time to gather her thoughts...

She remembered sitting there in the living room...waiting. She twirled the ring around her left finger absentmindedly as she watched the phone, willing it to ring. It had been two hours since he called last and told her that he had spun out. She had dialed his number but he hadn't answered. She figured he was trying to stay focused on the road. He didn't have his Bluetooth because it was blinking at her from the sofa table nearest the entry door.

It was just dawn and the sun was about to rise. The day was going to be overcast and cloudy. Surprisingly, she heard a bird chirping. "Silly bird," she thought to herself. "Why aren't you headed south like the rest of the birds?"

She looked out the window at the fresh layer of snow from last night. It was so clean and pure; just like Carter. It was amazing to her how perfect he was. Yes, he was still a man and yes they had problems but none that couldn't be solved and worked out.

She couldn't remember a time when they had actually argued other than the incident with Kim. They talked out their differences. Never once had he raised his voice at her. He was a man with no past, there was nothing to come back and haunt them. He always said he lived his life in such a way that he would never have any regrets.

The snow glistened as the tiny specks of sunshine hit it. It was a beautiful sight. She was going to hate to give up the condo but Carter said they needed something bigger, something they could raise a family in.

The thought of having his babies made her smile. She could just imagine him with a baby girl. He would spoil the baby to death just like he spoiled her.

He had recently come home one night slamming things around. She was upstairs in the bed and jumped up to see what the problem was.

"Carter, what is wrong with you?" she asked as she watched him tossing things around as if it wasn't 4'oclock in the morning and the things that he were throwing weren't fragile.

"Nothing Audrey. Just go back to sleep," he said in a tone that she had never heard come from his mouth.

"Excuse me? I think I deserve an explanation as to why you are acting a damn fool," she said in battle mode.

"I don't want to talk about it, okay. Just leave me alone, alright?" he said walking into the living room.

"You know what? Fine, I'm going back to bed. Deal with it on your own," she said walking back up the stairs.

"That's my fucking job!" he screamed. "I did all I could do. Why did they drive her? Why didn't they call the damn paramedics? They could have helped her!" he screamed punching the wall.

"Carter, baby. What happened? Please, baby let me help you," Audrey said easing down the stairs.

"I tried to help her Audi, but it was too late," he cried.

She hugged him around his waist and could feel the hot, wet tears soaking her hair as he leaned into her. He slowly sank to the ground still holding her as he went down. They ended up on the floor in the middle of the kitchen. She laid his head down on her lap.

"I did everything I could do. Why the fuck would they have a pitbull around a two year old?" he sobbed.

A terrible feeling grew in the pit of her stomach as she listened to him.

He took a few minutes to get himself together and told her that he had lost a two year old little girl named Anna that morning that had been mauled by the family dog that happened to be a pitbull. He had never lost a patient and for the first to be a child was extra hard on him.

They talked for hours that night until he finally fell asleep. He slept for five hours and was gone before she woke the next morning to do another 18 hour shift at his home away from home. He never mentioned the incident again. There were others after Anna, but none that touched him like she did.

"Come on Carter, call me baby," she said out loud to the empty house.

She got up and busied herself by dusting the already clean living room. She made sure the house phone was plugged in and checked the battery bars on her cell phone. When she couldn't think of anything else to do, she just...waited.

***

Carter pulled up at the gas station and got out to stretch his long legs. Mike made his way to the restroom while Carter looked around the gift shop.

He grabbed a Red Bull energy drink and a bag of chips. He leafed through a few magazines and then stopped at the rack that held the postcards. He grabbed a blank one and went up to the counter. He was about to pay for his items until he saw a key chain that he had to get. It was a sapphire blue Jaguar. That was Audrey's dream car. He'd promised that he would get it for her one day and he knew she would get a kick out of this. He added that to his bill and asked the clerk for a pen.

He grabbed his bag and moved over to the free space on the counter. He turned the card to the blank side and wrote a short poem to express his love for the love of his life.

While he was reading it over the female clerk interrupted him, "Sir, the mailman comes by here to pick up our mail around 11. If you want to buy a stamp from me, I'll mail that for you."

"You know what? I sure will buy a stamp. That's really nice of you to offer," he said taking out 44 cents from his pocket. "Thanks a lot. My fiancée is going to love it. She's a softy at heart."

"Not the Audrey I know," said Mike coming up to the counter. She's a pitbull in a skirt!"

They all laughed. Carter described how small she was in stature and the clerk laughed even harder.

"But that's my baby. Speaking of, come on man so I can get back to her," Carter said pushing Mike out the door.

The clerk read the card and sighed, "I wish I had a man like that."

Outside at the car, Carter had started to get back in the driver's seat.

"Naw man! You've been driving all this time. Let me take over," Mike argued.

"Really man, I'm straight. I know you been cutting hair all day and you look tired. I got in an hour or so at the crib so I'll take it on in," Carter insisted. He knew that Mike was really tired and he was too, but he felt like he could make it down there.

"Look man, I'm driving! Get your ass in the passenger seat. We only have about an hour to go now anyways. You let me get that little nap in so I'm ready," Mike said taking the keys out of Carter's hand.

Carter looked up in the sky at the huge flakes that were steadily falling. He noticed that the wind had picked up, too. He would have much rather driven himself but he resigned to letting Mike take it on in.

***

A Pepsi truck pulled back onto the freeway at the exit that Mike and Carter had missed a mile back. The driver, Matthew Long, had been on the road for 18 hours. He had pulled up at the gas station to buy another cup of coffee. He was trying to make it to the next truck stop where he would finally pack it in and take a nap for a few hours.

He had been driving for 12 years and weather like this didn't bother him. He turned on his soft rock station on XM satellite radio and he was good to go. He had his black coffee and pushed the pedal to the metal. He was at 65mph in less than a minute.

***

Mike pulled out of the gas station parking lot cautiously. He hadn't realized how slippery it really was when Carter had been driving. He didn't want to let on to Carter how nervous he was. He fiddled with the I-pod that was connected to the radio system and found some Jay-Z to ride to.

"Did you see this?" Carter said holding up the little blue car.

"What's that for?"

"My baby. I promise you, this is going to be the gift I give her at the wedding. What my baby wants, my baby get," he said proudly.

Mike shook his head as he approached the sign that read: Chicago. He slowly picked up speed getting onto the entry ramp.

"Give me that!" he said jovially while snatching the keychain and putting it in his pocket. "You are soooo lame, man! She's really got you whipped!"

***

Matthew was back in the groove as he listened to a Barry Manilow song. The smooth sound coming from Barry's mouth and the methodic swish-swash of the huge windshield wipers was so relaxing. He didn't realize that he had nodded off until the blistering hot coffee spilled into his lap.

"Shit!" he said as he jerked back awake. He reached for the cup, letting go of the steering wheel of the Mack truck.

"Damn it!" he yelled grabbing a hold of the wheel as the 18-wheeler swerved over to the other lane. He had to try to get the back of the truck out of the jackknife he was sliding into. For the first time in 12 years he had lost control of his truck!

***

"You really love that girl don't you?" Mike asked.

"Man, you just don't even know. That's my destiny. I love her so much," Carter said.

Mike pulled out onto the freeway just as he noticed an 18-wheeler swerving out of his lane. No other vehicles were on the road at the time...as destiny would have it.

"Oh shit!" he said not sure which side to pull on as the truck swerved cantankerously in and out of its lane.

Everything was happening so fast but for the Mike and Carter, life was in slow motion. Mike saw the 18 wheeler steadily approaching at an alarming speed in his rearview. Trying to make a blink of an eye decision, he swerved his wheel to the left in attempts to miss the imminent accident. Unfortunately, the foreign car's traction system kicked in and caused the rear end to fish tail with all the wet snow underneath the tires.

Mike looked at Carter with the most horrific feeling in his stomach. He shouted to Carter but it seemed as if the world was put on mute. Carter looked at Mike then back at the truck that was quickly gaining ground in his passenger window. He felt a calming sensation come over him and heard a voice speak. "Carter, come with me…"

***

The truck driver had no control over the 18 wheeler as it slid on the slippery sheets of new ice. He grabbed hold of the steering wheel tightly and locked his arms. He said a quick prayer and clenched his teeth as his fog lights were pointing directly onto the passenger side of the silver BMW that had spun out in front of him. Seconds before impact, the truck driver could see three bodies in the vehicle.

***

Carter squinted as the head light of the semi trucks beamed on his side of the car. He could barely hear the screams coming from Mike as he felt his whole body go numb.

"Oh my GOD, I'm about to die…" his mind told him. "Audrey! She'll never forgive me. I promised her that I would be back, and that I would never leave her…Damn."

Just before impact, Mike attempted to loosen his seatbelt and cover Carter. As he yanked for dear life on the belt, it wouldn't budge. For some strange reason, Mike's seatbelt didn't unlock, keeping him in restraints. All he managed to say was, "Carter! I'm sorry man…I'm…"

Carter never closed his eyes as he stared into the blinding lights that were aimed directly at him. Again, and for the final time he heard a subtle voice speak to him. "Take my hand, it is time…"

The impact from the crash buckled the 18 wheeler, forcing the tail end to separate and jackknife to the other side of the freeway. The truck itself careened into the passenger side of the vehicle, crushing it like a Pepsi can.

The snowflakes continued to fall like feathers from the sky. There was an eerie silence as the two mangled automobiles settled. The only thing moving was the spinning wheels of the now upturned semi-truck. The BMW was smashed into the median.

It would be more than ten minutes that slowly crept by before another lone vehicle struggling through the treacherous weather would reach them. The driver quickly pulled to the shoulder and ran down to the crash. At first glance, it looked as if there weren't any survivors…until he heard faint moans from the demolished BMW.

Within minutes there was organized chaos on the highway. Rescue vehicles, fire trucks and state police cars were everywhere.

After all of the twisted metal and debris were pulled apart, the emergency life rescue units were able to resuscitate one of the passengers from the car. He was flown by medi-vac to the University of Michigan where a special team of doctors worked fervently for hours on the one surviving victim from the BMW.

***

Not long after, every news reporter in the state was at the scene of the accident. The snow still fell heavily and traffic was delayed for hours. One reporter interviewed the truck driver as he was being carted away on a stretcher.

"Mr. Long, are you okay? Are you able to speak with us?"

"I'll be alright, my arm is broken, but I'm okay. I'm really worried about the passengers in the other car, please tell me they survived!"

The female reporter hung her head low and informed the truck driver that she couldn't issue out that type of information. The truck driver read between the lines and began to whimper.

"No, no! Tell me they made it! Tell me all three made it!"

The reporter was confused. From the report, it had been said that two males were inside of the vehicle at the time of the crash.

"Mr. Long, there were only two people in the vehicle, not three, according to the state trooper I just spoke with," the reporter said dubiously. She was asking for insight and stating it for confirmation as she walked briskly alongside the stretcher.

Adamantly, the truck driver shouted as he wiped tears away from his eyes with his good hand, "NO! There were three people inside! I saw them! I saw them with my own eyes!!!"

The reporter shook her head then chalked it up to the truck driver being delusional after such a traumatic experience. She watched as he was loaded into the EMS and walked away.

State troopers and county police were all over the crash site. As they sifted through the snow for evidence, one state trooper came across something sitting on top of snow. It was Carter's wallet. As he went through it, he saw a donor card. The state trooper rushed over to his squad car and called in the status of the two men along with giving them the ID number on the card.

Chapter 12

Dionne was still applying her makeup as Audrey continued to think about that day…

As she waited at the window like a little girl waiting for her Daddy to arrive home, a feeling of dread came over her body. She had to be mistaken but it felt as if someone or something had wrapped their arms around her. For a split second she felt as if she was being hugged. She stood up and checked to see if the window was cracked because she felt a blast of cold air in the room. She went into the dining room trying to shake that eerie feeling off that she felt.

She was still waiting two hours later and Carter wasn't answering his phone. She dialed it one last time and got the voicemail again. She tried Mike's phone and it went straight to voicemail.

She went in the kitchen and made herself a cup of coffee then returned to her spot on the couch. She grabbed his photo album from the end table and thumbed through it.

She couldn't help but laugh at all the candid's he'd taken of her. There was one when he caught her brushing her teeth. Another with her asleep, her cooking dinner, on the phone, she was never safe from his annoying lens.

"Something is wrong, I know it. He wouldn't go this long without calling me. He knows I'm worried. He wouldn't do this," she told herself.

Finally she couldn't deal with it alone anymore. She called Mrs. Bradford and told her what was going on.

"When was the last time you talked to him?" his mother asked.

"It was earlier this morning like around three o'clock. He hasn't called back yet and I'm really worried about him," she said trying her best to hold back the tears.

"Okay, I'm on my way. Just try to stay calm. He's okay. There's a reasonable explanation as to why he isn't calling, trust me," his mother said more to pacify herself.

Mrs. Bradford knew her son and inconsiderate was one thing he was not. There is no way that he would have left Audrey worrying about him. She knew that something was wrong. She only prayed that it wasn't that bad.

Audrey had made two similar phone calls to Alyssa and Monique and they both had come to wait it out with her as well.

The ladies sat around the island in the kitchen making small talk and watching the phones. The worry was beginning to show on Mrs. Bradford's face. Audrey had never seen her anything but poised and that was scaring the hell out of her.

It was 11o'clock when her phone finally rang. She jumped to answer when she saw his name pop up on the screen.

"It's him!" she screamed. "Baby? Where are you? Why haven't you been answering the phone? You scared the hell out of me! I thought something had happened to you," she screamed into the phone.

The voice that answered wasn't Carter. It was that of a sullen police officer. "Is this Audrey?"

"Ye-yes. Who is this? Where is Carter?"

"Ma'am, I called your number because Dr. Bradford was smart enough to put ICE behind your name, so we knew to call you in case of an emergency…"

Audrey interrupted, "Where is he? Is he ok?"

"Audrey, please…I need you to have a seat. There's been an accident."

"Ok. That's fine but how is Carter? Is he ok?" she asked desperately.

"Audrey, Dr. Bradford was killed earlier in a car accident on I-94."

The police officer was still talking but all Audrey was hearing was white noise. As the words registered in her brain, the color drained from her face. She dropped the phone and screamed, "Noooooo! Please no! Please no!"

Mrs. Bradford picked up the phone and identified herself. The police officer filled her in on the details of the accident while Monique and Alyssa tried to console Audrey.

Mrs. Bradford finished the call and sat back down at the island. With a stoic look on her face she delivered the news to the ladies. Her son, her sweet, sweet son was dead.

Chapter 13

"Excuse me for a minute Dionne. I just need a minute," Audrey said getting up and going into the bathroom. She hurried across the room as the other girls watched her. She just needed to be alone for a minute.

Even though it had been three years, the pain was still fresh. Every time she thought of him it was like pouring alcohol in an open wound.

She sat down on the small couch that was housed inside the enormous bathroom. There was a floor to ceiling sized mirror across from her. She stared at the reflection that was staring back at her. The waterproof mascara was now running down her cheeks like rivers of dirty water. The pain in her eyes was evident. She had lost her soul mate on that fateful day in November.

"Why Lord? Why did you have to take him away from me? I loved him so much. I needed him, Lord," she cried to herself.

What had she done in her life to deserve this? She couldn't fathom what she could have done for the Lord to take away the best thing that had ever happened to her.

The days after the accident were terrible for Audrey. Her doctor had her taking valium and she literally didn't get out of the bed or accept any visitors for three days. She was fine with the company of his scent on her pillow. She sat in his closet and cried for hours. The photo album had been the only thing helping her maintain her sanity. She literally felt empty, like a shell. There was a huge piece missing from her very being and she wished that she had been there with him.

It killed her to imagine him in pain all alone. She looked down at the picture that he had taken of her sleeping on his chest and wondered what he was thinking at that very moment. What were his last thoughts? Were they of her?

After three days of isolation, Alyssa and Austin came over and demanded that she at least get out of the bed to shower.

After an hour long shower, she sat back in the same spot where she had waited for his call.

"Audi, I know this is hard for you, baby. We all are so sad. We're here for you though. Mrs. Bradford was trying to call you, the funeral is Saturday," Alyssa said softly.

"Here's your mail Audrey," Austin said setting the huge pile of mail in her lap.

"I don't think I can go to the funeral, Alyssa. I really don't know if my heart can stand it," she said sifting through the envelopes.

Crying had become such the norm that she didn't realize that tears were falling from her eyes until she saw the water stain on the postcard on top of the pile of mail.

"Chicago?" she said picking the card up. She gasped as she immediately recognized his sloppy handwriting:

If sickness strickens you, then it will stricken me and I will be your support because your love strengthens me. If poverty bears upon me, I'm ok because your love enriches me and I look forward to the better days so that my love can manifest in all the ways...as a husband should to his wife. And if life took a turn for the worse, I'll never leave you, as my love will wait patiently for the rebirth. I'm in love with you, undeniably. I love loving you and I feel your essence loving me. – Carter

"He said he would never leave me," she said to no one in particular. Austin felt the lump growing in his throat as he tried to maintain his composure for his sister. He sat down on the couch next and hugged her.

"It's gonna be okay, Audrey. You know he's watching over all of us. I guess heaven needed him more than we did," he said rubbing her back.

The day of the funeral the three siblings stood as a united front as people lined up for their two minutes to speak kindly of the man that had touched so many hearts.

When it was Audrey's turn, Austin helped her to the podium and squeezed her hand to let her know he was there for her. She smiled, nodded then proceeded to speak.

"Finding a true, soulful love is such a rarity. Almost like finding a needle in a haystack. I was one of the lucky few to find that needle. Our connection defied time. There were moments when I felt like I had already reached forever. Carter was my soul mate. He mirrored me, showing me what I needed to do to better myself and helped me along the way. He was an angel that facilitated evolution in everyone's life that he touched. I am so blessed to have shared the time that I did with him and will treasure that time for the rest of my days. He may be gone from here but he will forever live in my heart."

She dabbed her eyes and accepted Austin's extended hand as he led her back to her seat.

After the funeral Mrs. Bradford came over and hugged Audrey tightly.

"You are still my daughter. Don't ever forget that. I also wanted to let you know that Carter was on the donor registry list. We donated all of his organs, so he will truly live on," Mrs. Bradford cried into Audrey's shoulder.

"Thanks Mom."

***

Audrey looked into the mirror wiping away the tears that still ran from that day. As she stood there in her undergarments with her running mascara, she had to laugh. She imagined Carter behind her with his camera ready to snap her in this somber but candid moment. Once the first giggle escaped she couldn't hold back the lava like laughter that poured out of her mouth.

"Do you hear that?" Shauntel said to the other ladies.

"Is that laughter?" Alyssa asked.

"Yes," laughed Monique. "That girl is laughing!"

Crystal knocked on the door of the bathroom and was met by a teary eyed Audrey with laughter bellowing from her tiny frame.

"Is this one of those gotta laugh to keep from crying moments?" Dana asked.

"Girl, he still makes me laugh, smile, love and live. I can't believe that I still have him in my life," Audrey said through her tears.

Their laughter and hugs were interrupted by the doors to the suite swinging open. They all abruptly turned around and were staring right smack at Inga Bergendorf.

"What, may I ask is going on in here? You ladies are on in one and a half hours. There is makeup to be done, dresses to be steamed. Come on! Chop! Chop!" she screamed as the ladies scrambled around the huge room.

Audrey scurried back over to Dionne so she could finally finish her make-up. She felt like the weight of the world had been lifted from her shoulders. She knew in her heart that Carter was happy for her. That he wanted her to be happy, to finally move on.

Mrs. Bradford came in the door as Dionne was finishing her makeup for the second time.

"Oh honey, you look beautiful," she said to Audrey who only had her undergarments on.

"Thanks Mom," Audrey said hugging the older woman. "Nervous?"

"You can't imagine! I've been crying all morning. I miss him so much. You know he still is right here," she said patting her heart.

"I know sweetie. We all miss him. But how lucky are you to have found love twice in a lifetime. Shane is a great man and if I had to have you with anyone other than my son, it would be him," Mrs. Bradford said with tears in her eyes. "Enough of that silliness, I came in here to give you these," she said putting a small black velvet bag in her hand.

"Your pearls? Ma, I can't take these. Mr. Bradford gave you these pearls," exclaimed Audrey pushing the bag back into her hand.

"I meant to say, you can borrow them for today. Is that better? This is your something borrowed, okay?" Mrs. Bradford insisted.

The pain was still evident in Mrs. Bradford's eyes and Audrey knew there was no way that she could refuse the precious gift.

"Of course they are. Thank you so much, Mom. Can you put them on for me?" Audrey asked turning her back so that Carter's mom could fasten the clasp.

"They're beautiful, just like you sweetie. Now go ahead and get ready and I'll see you in a minute."

The woman was the epitome of pride and elegance as she turned gracefully and walked out of the dressing room.

Audrey sighed and laid her hand over the pearls and felt even closer to Carter and his family.

"As fate would have it..."
Pt. 2

Something Old...Something New

Chapter 14

Three years prior...

"Over here, man! Over here!" Shane screamed to his teammate as they ran a pick and roll. The man passed the ball and Shane took off down the court. He was in the best shape he had ever been in his life. He was taking a kickboxing class, working out three days out of the week and playing these guys every Tuesday night. At 36 he was still able to school the young guys he was playing against now. It was evident in his crossover that they couldn't hang with him.

He unzipped his hoodie as he realized he had started to sweat. For it to be mid-November he was burning up! He chalked it up to all the running he was doing. He was a little winded but he still threw the ball into play. The rest of the guys ran down the court but his stride had slowed up significantly. He was suddenly short of breath and felt like he was being smothered. His hands began to shake. His left arm was tingling and he was starting to feel nauseated. He pulled back when a sharp pain shot through his chest.

"Arghh!" he screamed dropping to his knees.

The other men on the court turned to see what the problem was. When they saw Shane on his knees they all ran back to him.

"Shane? Shane, man, can you hear me?" his best friend Devin screamed.

Shane tried to reply but nothing was coming out. His eyes fluttered as he desperately tried to keep them open but he couldn't do that and try to breathe at the same time. He closed his eyes and tried to concentrate on breathing. He could faintly hear someone yell, "Someone dial 9-1-1!"

Then there was silence...and darkness.

Chapter 15

It had only been three weeks when Audrey got the names of the recipients of Carter's organs. She had made sure that Mrs. Bradford let her know. Lance had argued for a minute saying it was too soon for her but Mrs. Bradford insisted that she be given the list.

Audrey wasn't surprised that they had been able to use every viable organ from Carter's body. He was the epitome of healthiness. She ran her finger down the line of names as if that would close the gap of unknown between them.

Carlton Jackson had received his kidneys. John Union had received his eyes. Adrienne Normandy had received one of his lungs. She folded the paper back up before reaching the end of the list. She was overwhelmed with grief again as the tears fell freely from her pained face.

This was so typical of Carter. He would give all of him to better someone else's life and in the end this is exactly what he had done.

She placed the paper inside her bible and put it in her drawer. She looked over to the cold side of the bed. She had refused to sleep in his spot because she didn't want the scent of him to leave. She slept in his t-shirts because it made her feel closer to him. She had yet to remove any of his belongings. By appearances, Carter was alive and well in the condo.

She walked over to the bathroom to get in the shower. His bathrobe still hung on the hook on the back of the door. His toothbrush still stood in the holder next to hers, as it always had.

She stepped into the shower and let the water run over her head. She had been wearing her hair pulled back into a ponytail so getting her hair wet was the least of her worries. The shower was her sanctuary. She pretended that the water washed away the sadness. She wished like hell that she could lather up and wash away the hurt and pain that she felt every single day.

After the water ran cold, she stepped out of the shower and was shocked to see writing on the steamed mirror. It read: Audrey and Carter forever. She stood with her mouth open because she had cleaned the bathroom and the mirror a few times since the accident. It wasn't logical for this to still be on the mirror.

She put her hand on the mirror to make sure this was real. Normally she would have been scared as hell but there was a feeling of calm and peace that drifted over her body. She knew it was him and was immediately comforted by his presence.

She dried her hair and went to watch their favorite movie which was ironically, "The Breakup," with Vince Vaughn and Jennifer Aniston.

Her phone buzzed next to her and she noticed it was Mike's number. He had been calling her for the past couple of weeks but she just couldn't do it. She couldn't talk to him. In her find, if he hadn't called Carter in that suicide mission, he would be lying there in her arms.

She fell asleep hugging Carter's bathrobe.

Something Old...Something New

Chapter 16

The months after the funeral all ran together for Audrey. She had finally allowed Lance and Austin to come go through his clothes and shoes. She said they could have everything except his Doctor's coat, a cashmere cardigan that he'd always worn and a few bottles of his cologne.

The dreams that kept her awake at night finally subsided. She had gotten used to the little things that started happening when she was there alone.

The kitchen light had flickered a few times when she walked in there at night for her midnight ice cream snack. She knew it was him. This was a ritual every night for them when Carter was alive. Whoever was still up had to bring the other person a bowl of their favorite flavor. His was pistachio and hers was rocky road. It was unfair that she had to make her own now and she really thought the flickering was him teasing her.

It had been six months since the accident and Audrey had almost forgotten about Mother's Day. She had gone to church and brunch with Alyssa, the kids and her Mom. She was headed over to Mrs. Bradford's to see her when Monique called her.

"Hey girl," she said answering the phone.

"How you doing? I was going to stop over there if you were home," Monique said.

She knew Mother's Day was hard for Mo because she had lost her mother to cancer in 2002 but it never got easier over the years. "I was about to go see Mrs. Bradford but I'll meet you there, Mo," Audrey said.

"Oh naw, girl. I was just near the house and was going to stop by. You go over there. She'll be happy to see you," Monique said trying not to sound disappointed.

"No really, Mo. I'm just around the corner. Go ahead to the house. I'll be there in five minutes tops," Audrey said lying. She was down the street from Mrs. Bradford's house and would be at least fifteen minutes.

She whipped a u-turn and almost hit a burgundy Mercedes SL500. The driver laid on the horn as she drove by. She flipped him the finger and kept driving even though she was 100% in the wrong.

She split the E.T.A. (estimated time of arrival) in half by speeding to her house. They popped open a bottle of Moscato and talked for two hours. They never touched on the subject of Auntie Monica or Carter though. Sometimes not saying anything at all is saying enough.

It was almost five o'clock when she made it back to Mrs. Bradford's house. She was surprised to see a Mercedes in the driveway.

"I know that is not the same Mercedes that I flipped off. Please say that is not the same car," she prayed walking up to the door. She rang the bell with her fingers crossed.

"Hey! Babygirl, how you been?" Lance said grabbing her in a bear hug.

She could barely talk as he had her face smashed into his chest. She was thankful though because he looked so much like Carter.

"Hey Lance," she said after he put her down. "I've been making it. How have you and your wife and kids been?"

Before he could answer the whole crew came running into the room embracing her. Finally, after she had hugged them all she walked into the living room and was surprised to see Mrs. Bradford sitting there with a very attractive gentleman.

"Yep, that's the guy that I flipped off," she thought to herself as she walked over to give Mrs. Bradford a hug.

"Audrey, honey. I'm so happy to see you, sweetie. I almost thought you weren't coming by," Mrs. Bradford said holding Audrey at an arm's length so she could look her over.

"I was here earlier but..." she caught herself as she noticed the disapproving look that the guy who was seated on the couch gave her. "Now you know I wouldn't dare not show up on a special day like today, Mom," she finished giving the guy her own disapproving look.

"Oh, I have a surprise for you," Mrs. Bradford said looking over to the guy. "I want to introduce you to someone..."

"I think we already met," the guy said standing and extending his hand to Audrey. "Shane Baldwin."

"Audrey Parchman," she said barely shaking his hand.

"You two know each other," Lance said with a look of astonishment on his face.

"Well, not really. Let's just say we almost had a run in before," Shane said taking a seat.

Audrey rolled her eyes and walked into the kitchen with the kids who had gone back to eating their ice-cream. She grabbed a bowl and joined them at the island in the kitchen.

"Auntie Audrey, when can we come over and play with the twins," Lily, the oldest girl asked.

"Whenever you're ready. Why don't we go to the water park for Memorial Day?"

"Yeah!" Lily and Laila screamed together.

"Then it's a plan. Lily, can you go out to my car and get that present in the back for Nana for me?" Audrey asked remembering the Waterford Vase that she had bought for Mrs. Bradford. "Be careful, Lily."

"Ok, Auntie Audrey," she said taking the keys.

When Lily came back in Audrey went to the living room and much to her dismay the stranger was still there. She waited patiently for a break in their conversation. While listening, she learned that he was an art dealer and a successful one it sounded like. He had just come back from an auction in Monaco where he had sold a $5 million dollar print.

"Excuse me Mom. I wasn't going to stay long. I wanted to give you this before I left," Audrey said handing her the gift.

"Oh thank you, sweetie," Mrs. Bradford said opening the gift. Audrey watched as she opened it, sneaking peeks at Shane to see his reaction.

"That's really beautiful," he said catching her looking at him.

"Thank you," Audrey said blushing.

"It is, Audrey. Thank you so much," Mrs. Bradford said. "Will you two excuse me for minute?" she said getting up and leaving the two sitting there.

"Let's call a truce," Shane said getting up and extending his hand out to her.

"I don't know what you're talking about," Audrey said stubbornly taking his hand in hers.

"You know exactly what I'm talking about, Ms. Flipping the Bird," he said laughing.

"Okay, I'm sorry," she said laughing. "So you're an art dealer. How exciting is that?" she said sarcastically.

"I've already heard you're a realtor, and how exciting is that?" he shot back with a grin.

"I'm making people's dreams come true," she said.

"And I'm helping people invest their money in a solid investment for the future and picking up a few pieces of my own on the way," he countered.

"So you travel a lot, I assume."

"When I want to. I've been taking it easy for the past 6 months though. This trip to Monaco was my first in over 8 months. It was worth it though," he said with a smile. "I needed the rest and needed to get away."

"I heard that. Sometimes I wish I could get away," she said drifting off.

"You can, all you have to do is do it," he said in his own daydream.

Mrs. Bradford walked into the room as the two wandered in their own private thoughts.

"So Shane, what's next? Paris, Rome?" Mrs. Bradford asked.

"No, I think I'm done for a minute. I need to catch up on some things around the house, as a matter of fact, I need to get your number Audrey because I have a few properties that I'm looking at possibly selling, if you don't mind," Shane asked looking at Audrey.

"Hmm? Oh, no I don't mind," she said taking her card holder out of her purse and handing him a card.

"Great. Well I think I've overstayed my welcome," he said rising up from the couch.

"You could never do that Shane. It's always a pleasure to see you. We're so glad that you reached out and contacted us," Mrs. Bradford said giving him a huge hug.

"I'm glad that you were open to meeting me. I'm so grateful to you and your family, Mrs. Bradford. Listen, I know I could never pay you back for what you've done for me but if there is ever anything that I can do for you, please don't hesitate to ask," he said heading for the door.

"I have to let you out," Audrey said just as her cell phone rang. It was Monique again and she was having a moment. Audrey kissed Mrs. Bradford and told her she would be back over soon.

"Audrey, I needed to talk to you," Mrs. Bradford said as she was walking out.

With the phone to her ear she mouthed, "I'll call you. I promise."

"It was nice meeting you," she said to Shane.

"I'll be in touch about those properties," he said.

She nodded, still trying to console Mo and get in her car simultaneously.

Chapter 17

A few weeks later Audrey and Alyssa were just sitting down at the movies when the strange number came across her Blackberry. She hit ignore figuring the person would leave her a message. She was surprised when the person called right back. Again she hit ignore and went back to watching the movie. The stubborn caller called back again so she excused herself past 6 people because they were seated in the middle of the row. A few disgruntled people hissed and moaned but she pushed her way past until she made it out to the aisle.

"Hello?" she whispered as she walked uphill to the double doors of the theater.

"Don't press ignore when I'm calling you. Especially when I know you aren't busy," the caller said.

"Who is this?" she said loudly and was met with a bunch of people, "Ssshhh'ing" her. "Who is this?" she whispered again.

"It's Shane. I've been calling you for two days and you haven't returned my calls. What kind of realtor are you?"

"Excuse me?" she said looking at the phone.

"You heard me and you got time to go to the movies but you can't call your clients back?" he said jokingly.

She noticed she was hearing an echo and turned to see him standing outside the door of the movie she had walked out of. She couldn't help but to smile as she hung up the phone.

"Very funny, Mr.?" she said forgetting his last name.

"Call me Shane and I thought so too," he said smiling back.

That's when she noticed how straight and white his teeth were. She also took in the fact that he was maybe 6"1, with beautiful cocoa colored skin and dark curly hair with deep dimples. He was dressed in a dark pair of jeans and a striped light blue and white button up shirt. His Polo baseball cap was pulled down low on his eyes almost hiding the most beautiful pair of brown eyes she'd seen in a long time.

"Hey Shane," she said extending her hand for a hand shake.

"Hey Audrey. What's a guy gotta do to get a meeting over coffee?"

"Just ask," she said feeling a little giddy inside. "I'm free tomorrow around ten if you are. We can meet at the Starbucks in Ferndale on Woodward."

"I'll be there. Don't be late and don't make any u-turns," he said smiling as he went back into the theater.

She followed behind him and noticed he sat down two rows in front of them. She found herself looking to see who he was with. There was a guy on one side and an empty seat then another guy and then a girl. The theater was packed so unless he was gay or just hanging with a homie, he was forced to sit where he had sat between the two guys.

"Why do I care?" she said to herself. Though she couldn't answer the question right away, she spent the rest of the movie happy that he wasn't with a woman.

When the movie was over she noticed him leaving...alone and he waved and said, "Tomorrow at 10. Don't forget."

"I won't," she said waving back.

"Damn, who is that?" Alyssa said.

"A potential client," Audrey said smiling at Alyssa's brazenness.

"Potential? You need to secure his ass. Sell him a house or something. That brotha is fine," Alyssa said.

"Girl, stop it. He's a friend of Mrs. Bradford's so don't get any crazy ideas, plus you know I ain't even thinking about a man," Audrey said.

"I didn't say marry him and I know you aren't looking for a man but you can't deny that the man is fine, now," Alyssa said smiling at her sister.

Audrey smiled slyly, "Yes, he is fine BUT I ain't thinking about him...like that." She hit the clicker to her car and they both got in.

The next morning, she was up by eight trying to find the right outfit to wear. She had pulled out a suit but decided against that. They were meeting at Starbucks not the office. She settled on jeans and a crisp white shirt with some nice sandals. She pulled her hair back into a sleek ponytail and grabbed her Navy Blue Berkin bag.

The sun was shining brightly and she was surprised to see a Blue Jay perched on a hanging branch of the old oak tree in front of the condo. Again the serene moment reminded her of Carter and how he would have ran to get his camera.

She threw her messenger bag and purse in the back seat of her car and put on her sunglasses as if to shield the world from the tears that she still cried. She took a few minutes before she pushed the start engine button in her car.

It was hard to believe it had been 7 months since the accident. It hadn't been easy for her at all. Everything reminded her of Carter. Smells, sounds, little things like the Blue Jay in the tree. He was everywhere around her. She smiled at the thought of him, even when she wanted to cry.

She pressed the button to start the car and made her way to her appointment. She thought about what Alyssa had said about Shane. He was definitely a looker but her heart remained with Carter. Though many men had stepped her way, she was in no shape to even think about dating anyone. It was just too soon. Besides, Mr. Shane hadn't even hit on her and she was already thinking of ways to dissuade him.

"How arrogant am I?" she said out loud in the car laughing at herself.

When she pulled up to the busy coffee house it was buzzing as usual with suburbanites willing to pay five bucks for the same old coffee. She was guilty of it too as she pulled her bags out and headed to the door.

She didn't even notice the double look she received from the gentleman that held the door open for her. Her mind was a hundred miles away...until she saw Shane.

The funny thing is as oblivious she was to all the stares she was getting from all the business men as well as a few women, it hit Shane in the face like a slap.

It struck him odd that the little feisty woman that had almost hit his car was as humble as a ladybug. She had no idea that she was as strikingly beautiful as she was. With her hair pulled back she only exposed the gem of a face she had. The high cheekbones, the almond shaped eyes, the heart shaped mouth and the flawless skin, all of it was exquisite.

He put that out of his mind as he approached her and guided her back to the table that he had been sitting at for 10 minutes.

"Hey. Am I late?" she asked taking a seat.

"No. I got here a few minutes early so I wouldn't miss my girlfriend," he said sitting down after she took a seat.

"Oh...okay," she said feeling her cheeks turning red.

"As a matter of fact, let me introduce you to her," Shane said standing again grabbing her hand.

Audrey followed clumsily as he pulled her over to a little old lady seated at the couches that were in the middle of the shop. She was sipping on a latte and her whole face lit up when she saw Shane approach her.

"Shane! Honey, it's so good to see you. I wondered if you were going to be here. You know I worry about you, sweetie," she said pulling him down to hug her.

"Mrs. Logan, you know I couldn't miss a week without seeing my girl. Don't you be worrying about me either, I'm fine. As a matter of fact, I want you to meet my friend Audrey. Audrey, this is Mrs. Logan," he said like he was presenting an award.

Audrey blushed again as she realized that Mrs. Logan was the girlfriend he was talking about and also took notice of his acknowledgment of their friendship, which she was unaware of.

"Hi, Mrs. Logan. It's a pleasure to meet you," Audrey said shaking the older woman's hand and then suddenly second guessing her choice of outfits.

"Oh, no sweetie, I get hugs," Mrs. Logan said pulling Audrey down to give her a hug.

Audrey laughed as she bent down to hug the seasoned belle. When they embraced she smelled the same perfume that her own grandmother used to wear. It took her back to Sunday mornings at church with her grandmother fanning herself with a church fan and pinching Alyssa, Audrey and Austin as they misbehaved.

"Shane, she's so pretty. Where did you find her?" Mrs. Logan said shifting in her seat to get a better look.

"I guess you can say we kinda bumped into each other," he said smiling at Audrey. "But I'm not going to take you away from your coffee with the ladies. I will see you next week."

It was only then that Audrey noticed the two other ladies sitting with Mrs. Logan.

"Take care of yourself Shane. It was really nice meeting you Audrey," Mrs. Logan said patting them both on their cheeks.

They took their seats back at the table. He smiled at her as she took out her notebook and got right down to business. Her face was flushed and there was a strand of hair that had come loose from her ponytail waving in the air. Even with that slight imperfection she was still gorgeous. He struggled to listen to her as she explained what she could do to help get rid of a few properties that he had no use for anymore. The beach houses in Maine and Miami, the loft in New York, the condo at Martha's Vineyard were all part of his past. A fast paced, living on the edge past that he no longer wanted any parts of.

Shane Baldwin had experienced every color, shape and flavor woman imaginable. A self-proclaimed 'bachelor for life', Shane always had a steady stream of women walking in and out of his door. There was a woman in each city at his disposal and he often times indulged. His mother had warned him that he needed to slow down but he was having too much fun; until he was forced to sit down.

"Shane? Mr. Baldwin?" Audrey said waving her hand in his face.

"Huh? Oh, I'm sorry," he said snapping out of his trance like state.

"I'm sorry I'm boring you," she said shuffling her papers.

"You're not boring me. I was just thinking..."

"Don't worry about it. Well, all we need to do now is sign the buyer agency agreement and I can get started listing your properties," she said again transitioning back to business.

"Yeah, that's no problem, just tell where to sign," he said.

"Sign here and here," she said putting X's where he needed to sign. "I appreciate your business. Any friend of Mrs. Bradford's is a friend of mine."

"Speaking of Mrs. Bradford, did she tell you how we met?" Shane inquired.

"No, as a matter of fact she didn't," Audrey said looking down at her watch. "Wow, I didn't know it was already eleven. I was talking your ear off, no wonder you fell asleep on me," she exclaimed getting up and grabbing her purse. Standing, Audrey extended her hand and continued, "Shane, you have my card if you have any other questions."

"I do have one more question. Would you mind having dinner with me tonight?" Shane asked watching for her reaction. He knew that this was a delicate situation and it needed to be handled with care.

"Dinner? Umm...well, I'm really not trying to date or anything right now," Audrey stammered.

"I didn't say a date...I just asked for dinner. Two people eating at the same place, right? We both have to eat, right? What do you say, about 7 o'clock? We can meet at the restaurant if that would make you feel better, *BUT* I'm too much of a gentleman for us to go dutch..." Shane said smiling.

Audrey laughed at his lame effort to make a chasm in his request. "I guess you're right. We both have to eat. I guess we can do that."

"I'll call you at 6 to confirm, okay?"

"Okay. Thanks for the coffee."

As she walked out of the Starbucks, there was a familiar feeling of calm that came over her. She decided to head into the office to take care of some paperwork that she had on her desk.

Chapter 18

It was 6:15 and Shane held his phone in his hand awaiting Audrey's confirmation phone call. He sat in his office and rotated two silver stress relieving balls while staring out of the wall to wall window. His view was blocked by the enormous skyscrapers adjacent to his own building. Shane decided to catch up on a little paperwork to pass time. His cell phone rang.

"Whassuppppp???" Devin screamed into the phone in his usual boisterous manner. "I'm hitting up the booby bar to watch the Finals tonight. You wit' it? A little basketball, with a little Roset, with a lot of ass shaking?"

"Naw, man. I'mma have to pass tonight," Shane said sitting back in the high back leather chair.

"Okay, the only thing that would make you pass on a lot of ass shaking is if you had one individual ass shaking for you already. Then she would have to be a helluva piece for you not to put that ass on hold," Devin explained. No one knew him better than Devin. They were the epitome of 'brothers from another mother'.

"This isn't just a piece of ass D. This one is special. It's crazy too because I felt it the first time I saw her," Shane got up and walked over to the huge window and peered out at the cityscape.

"Hello? Is this Shane Baldwin? Oh, forgive me. I must have the wrong number," Devin joked. 'What has gotten into you, bro?"

"Man, I can't explain it. I mean by appearances, she is one of the most beautiful women I've ever seen. She's a little feisty but that's cool. I know she is hurting and that's part of it. When I saw her I wanted to comfort her. Man, it's crazy how I'm drawn to her."

"Is this the one…" Devin started.

"Yes, and I don't want to hear it. I already know," Shane interrupted.

"Man, you need to tell her right away. Don't play with that girl's feelings. You of all people know how that feels. I'm not going to lecture you because I got some ass waiting on me. Do the right thing, bro," Devin said hanging the phone up.

As soon as he sat the phone down on the desk it rang again.

"Hello, Shane?" asked a sweet voice.

His face lit up with excitement as the wait was over. He felt silly sitting there with butterflies in his stomach.

"Heyyy Audrey, are we still on for today?"

"Yes, Shane...we are. Uhm, do you have somewhere specific in mind?"

"As a matter of fact, I do. Meet me at the Shark Bar, or would you prefer I send one of my cars for you?"

Though flattered by his offer, Audrey kindly declined. That was a bit much for her at the time and it would have felt more of a date than a business meeting. She was in no shape to start dating again. Audrey barely made it through the day completing the basic functions.

They agreed to meet at the restaurant at a 7 o'clock.

"Wow, you look great Audrey...Hey, I like that dress...You smell delicious..." Shane practiced his opening line in the mirror as he adjusted his tie.

"No, that sounds so weak!" he laughed to himself. After sighing he continued, "Nah, I'll just say what I feel when I see her, life isn't rehearsed."

Audrey arrived at the restaurant wearing a black wrap around dress with four inch black heels. Her hair was swept up into a loose ponytail with wispy pieces falling from the crown. She looked gorgeous.

The greeter at the door escorted her to the table where Shane was already waiting. As she saw him in the distance, she noticed how handsome he was. She hadn't allowed herself to see past the pain in her own heart, let alone the goodness in any other person's heart.

Shane became instantly nervous with goose bumps all over as he stood to shake Audrey's hand.

Audrey frowned at the comfortable and cozy booth that was almost detached from the rest of the restaurant. It was for VIP's and other high status folk. The setting was more of a romantic atmosphere than Audrey would have preferred. In her mind, she wished that they could sit at a table.

Shane held her elbow as she bent to scoot over into the booth. She slid over into the booth and set her purse in between them. Shane scooted in close to Audrey, invading more of her personal space than she would have rather shared.

She snuck a glance at him as he perused the wine menu. He was so handsome. It wasn't just his looks though. It was the way he carried himself. She took notice of the chivalry that he displayed.

He was dressed in a pair of jeans with a blazer and a pair of loafers. She looked at his neatly kept nails and subconsciously looked for 'the ring'. She'd heard plenty of horror stories and definitely didn't want any drama. She made it up in her mind that this was simply a friendly dinner and she would relax and enjoy herself.

They talked over a glass of wine before they ordered and she learned that he was fluent in French. What he didn't know was that she was as well.

The French waiter walked over to the table and Shane greeted him by name, "Pierre, Comment fortuné dois-je avoir une si belle dame avec moi ce soir?

Audrey giggled to herself as she listened to Shane ask the waiter, "How lucky was he to have such a beautiful lady with him tonight?"

Pierre answered, "Mr. Baldwin, jamais vu vous avec une femme sans attrait mais celui-ci est extraordinaire, je dois dire."

Shane smiled and nodded his head in agreement.

"Really?" She thought to herself, "So he always has beautiful women, but I'm different." It was time to bust up their secret conversation.

"Well Pierre, dites à M. Baldwin qu'il a extrêmement de la chance parce que les dates de dîner comme moi viennent seulement une fois dans une vie!" she said laughing at the surprised look on their faces.

"Really Ms. Parchman? I'm lucky because dinner dates like you only come once in a lifetime, huh?" Shane said admiring her even more. "I wonder what else you are hiding. Can you sing or something?"

"That was it. The talent stops there," Audrey laughed feeling even more comfortable. The wine had loosened her up a bit as well.

They talked over an hour before they decided to order. He kept her laughing with his horrific dating stories, his college days in Omega Psi Phi, and his Mama's boy stories.

"I can't believe you sucked your thumb until you were twelve! Your teeth are perfect," Audrey said laughing at him once again.

"Yep, until I got interested in girls and found something else to suck on," he said looking mischievous as he blinked his eye at her.

"Hmm. I wonder what?"

"I'll tell you exactly what it was...apple jolly ranchers," he said.

"Jolly ranchers?"

"Yep. My first girlfriend, Cassandra Evans worked at her parent's penny candy store and she used to give me jolly ranchers all the time. That kept me with her and my thumb out of my mouth. So it was a win-win, for a while," Shane said drinking down the last sip of wine from his glass.

"What about you?" he asked. "Who was your first love?"

Audrey swirled the blood colored wine around in her glass. She waited before she answered because she'd never really thought about it before.

"Shane, my first and last love was one in the same. I don't think I'll ever love anyone like I loved him," she said looking him deep in the eyes. She smiled as an image of Carter appeared in the forefront of her mind.

Shane noticed the look on her face and figured it might not be a good time to broach the subject that he had been trying to bring up to her for weeks. The same subject that Devin had so 'subtly' reminded him not to forget.

It was too soon to spring something on her with such magnitude behind it. He wasn't sure how she was going to take it. He had convinced Mrs. Bradford to let him tell her. He decided to wait until the moment was right.

"So tell me about your family," Shane inquired trying to change the subject.

"Well there isn't much to tell. I have an older sister and a younger brother who I am very close to. My mom lives out in Troy and kinda keeps to herself. I have a really close knit group of friends and a cousin that I love a bunch. Of course the Bradford's, they're my...uh...extended family," she said. "What about yours?"

"I'm an only child. My parents live in Boca Raton, and they both were only children so I don't have any uncles, aunts or cousins. Isn't that crazy?"

"Wow, no cousins?"

"Nope. There's Devin who I've known for as long as I can remember. He's my best friend and the closest thing to a brother I can get. The dude is so crazy, he'll have you rolling on the floor laughing. I always tell him he should have been a comedian. With his sense of humor you would never guess he's an accountant. You'll meet him one day," Shane said taking a slice from the piece of cheesecake that Pierre had set between them.

"Sounds like a great guy," she said indulging on the dessert as well. "Cheesecake is the one vice I can't resist."

"He really is. I used to call him my conscience. He keeps me on the right track," Shane laughed pushing the dessert closer to her.

Audrey laughed as she was reminded of her relationship with a few of her friends.

They traded college stories over the rest of dessert and were having so much fun they didn't realize the restaurant was almost empty. Audrey looked at her watch with tears in her eyes from laughing, "Wow, Shane, it's almost eleven o'clock."

"Time flies when you're having fun."

"You're right. I guess it does," she said smiling at him. "I guess we should be leaving." She took the napkin out of her lap and set it on the table.

"I hate for the night to end but I know you have meetings and I have a few things to do tomorrow as well so Cinderella, let me escort you to your carriage," he said holding out his hand to help her out of the booth.

"Au revoir, Pierre," they both said.

"Au revoir, Mr. Baldwin et son joli compagnon," Pierre replied.

"Pierre, you're too kind," Audrey said blushing.

As they approached her car, she thanked him for dinner.

"It was my pleasure, really. Hopefully we can do it again soon," Shane said sincerely.

"That would be nice," she replied getting into her car.

On the drive home, she went over the evening. There was something different about him. He was handsome and obviously well off. How come he didn't have a girlfriend or a wife? He'd made sure to emphasize that a few times during their conversation.

She couldn't help but acknowledge the beautiful personality he had. He was the perfect gentleman, well educated and he spoiled himself rotten. He spoke highly of his mom which is always a plus because the way a man treats his mother is usually indicative of how he treats other women.

She had really enjoyed the hours spent with him. She settled in for the night because there was a mountain of paperwork on her desk at the office that she vowed to conquer tomorrow.

She picked up her journal and started to write:

June 12, 2009

Hey, today was a good day. I met with a client and we ended up going to dinner. He is a really nice guy Carter. Don't worry though, I'm not stepping out on you, baby. I told him that you were my first and my last love. I miss you so much. Not a day goes by that I don't think of you. You are my everything, baby. I will love you forever.

Audi

She dreamed of Carter all night long and woke up to a tearstained pillow.

Chapter 19

The next day she was sitting at her desk when the receptionist rang in on her phone.

"Audrey, there's a package for you up front," Alexis chirped into her intercom.

"Thanks Alexis. I'll be right up," she said pushing her chair back and stretching. She looked out the window happy to see the sun shining brightly. There wasn't one cloud in the sky.

"I think I'm going to go jogging when I go home," she thought as she walked up front to claim her package.

She grabbed the box and thanked Alexis. It wasn't the package she was expecting. She was waiting on a purchase agreement from a client that should have come via FedEx. She closed the door to her office and sat back down at her desk.

The label only read her name she noticed as she opened the small box. Inside was a fork, a napkin and a folded note that read:

"Come join me for cheesecake at the picnic table out back. You can't say no, because you said you can't resist cheesecake. I'll be there at 12:30. Don't be late. – Shane"

She smiled as she looked out the window at the Blue Jay that was sitting on her window ledge. The bird was chirping some crazy bird song almost if it was challenging her to take Shane up on his offer.

At 12:25 she sat at the picnic table alone taking in the scenery. A few of the agents were sitting on the rolling hill that served as the 'backyard' of the agency. She watched with envy, Gene and Laura who were carrying on the 'forbidden' office romance. Though neither was married, everyone dissuaded them from working with their lover.

"I would have given anything to spend every waking moment with Carter. Granted he would have had to sell real estate because I wouldn't have had the patience for all that schooling," she said laughing out loud.

Walking up behind her, Audrey felt Shane's presence even before he spoke, "You started the party without me?"

"Nah, I was just thinking," she said turning to face him.

"Thanks for joining me," he said placing the wicker picnic basket on the bench next to her. He pulled from the basket a red and white gingham tablecloth and spread it over the table. He placed a boxed caramel cheesecake on the table with two plates and flatware.

"This is not good. Cheesecake two nights in a row is knocking me way off my diet," Audrey digressed with a mouthful of cheesecake.

"Don't worry, we'll work it off tonight," Shane said as he poured her a cup of Hazelnut espresso from a thermos.

"Excuse me?" she said putting her cup down.

"The gym...I was going to invite you to go to the gym with me tonight," he said snickering at her.

She felt her cheeks turning rosy. She playfully hit him on the arm.

"Well, what did you think I was talking about?" he asked.

"Whatever! Just cut the cake, alright?"

They spent the next hour talking about his childhood and how lonely it was being an only child. He recalled how he surrounded himself with friends of all kinds. "I pretty much had two of everything so my friends could play as well. Needless to say my house was the place to be on the block. My mother may have only given birth to one child but she had many children," he said picking a leaf out of her hair that gotten caught.

She was mesmerized by his voice. There was something calming, even soothing about his voice. He had the voice of a storyteller so she was easily engrossed into every word that he said. Listening to him talk became something that she needed every day, so they talked on a daily basis and saw each other for lunch or dinner at least twice a week.

Though the attraction was apparent they never broached the subject of dating or sex. Neither of them inquired about the others lives other than what was shared when they were together.

They spent the summer boating on his yacht, bike riding, jet skiing and horseback riding. He had invited her on a business trip to Montreal and it was the first time that she declined any of his invitations. She didn't want to tempt fate.

August 11, 2009

Hey sweetie. Shane and I spent the day relaxing at the condo. He helped me with the yard which I have totally been neglecting. He's a really good guy. I don't know what it is but I'm drawn to him. I feel bad because I feel like I benefit so much more from our friendship than he does. I feel at peace when he is around and surprisingly enough, he reminds me of you. His gestures and even the way he tilts his head when he talks to me reminds me of just how you used to be.

He is so much like you. He likes nasty pistachio ice cream, loves his parents to death, he is an animal lover and he is probably number one on every friends speed dial. The male "Dear Abby" is what I call him.

It's scary sometimes because I feel your presence whenever he is around me. So, I selfishly keep him close to me. Good thing he seems to want to hang around. I love you forever - Audi

Monique, Alyssa and Shauntel were all surprised when they found out how much time Audrey and Shane were spending together. Although they were just friends, it was obvious to everyone that they were crazy about each other.

When she invited Shane to the annual Labor Day BBQ they all were floored. The gang watched as the two sat talking and laughing.

"She's totally in love with him," Shauntel whispered to Alyssa.

"In love? I don't think so. She's only known him for a couple of months plus her guard is up so high he would have to be an Olympic pole vaulter to get over the wall she's built. I think she just enjoys spending time with him, though I must say if she doesn't want him I would definitely step up and take one for the team," Alyssa said looking over at Shane who was dressed in a tan linen short set and a pair of brown Gucci moccasins. His dark curly hair was freshly tapered and his goatee shown with a deep sheen that only accented his perfectly straight white teeth. His dimples were displayed as he and Audrey shared a private joke.

"He is one fine brother. Audrey never has a problem catching a fine man. I like him for her though. He's really nice. He reminds me of..."

"Carter," the ladies said together.

"I don't know about that," Monique said walking up to Alyssa and Shauntel. "But I can say I haven't seen her smile this much since Carter was alive. I asked her if she gave him any yet..."

"No you didn't Mo," Alyssa said putting her hand over her mouth.

"Yes, I did. I can't see them getting on like they are without them having gotten busy," she said with her hand on her hip.

"You know you are something else Mo," Shauntel said taking a bite out of her hot dog.

The three girls looked on as Audrey and Shane yelled for the next spade partners to play 'Rise and Fly'. They were undefeated in not only the card game but life itself.

Chapter 20

Shane dialed Audrey's phone for the fifth time only to get the voicemail again. He knew what she was doing but he wasn't going to allow her to deal with it on her own. She needed him and he knew that he needed her, too.

He looked out the window surprised to see the first snow falling. They had an unusually warm Thanksgiving and the last thing they expected to see three days later was snow. He hit the remote starter button on his key ring and heard his SUV engine roar to life.

He had never popped up over her house but that day was different. He had talked to the girls and they all had decided to let her take that day for herself. Alyssa had at least talked to her that morning so he knew that she was breathing. He probably should have followed suit and left her alone but he needed to see her for himself.

As he drove to her condo he could almost feel his heart beating through his coat. He wasn't sure if she would let him in. She had every right to deal with it all alone but if they hadn't developed anything else they were definitely friends that were there for each other.

He pulled up to her garage and hopped out. It had started getting dark earlier and she hadn't turned on any lights in the house. As Shane approached, he saw the dim flicker of the flames from the fireplace in the den through the window.

He rang the bell and waited for a response. No response. He knocked and knocked harder while calling out her name. She still didn't answer. He literally laid on the doorbell for five minutes until finally, she snatched open the door with a ferocious look of an angered lioness on her face.

"WHAT IS IT SHANE?!!!"

"Why aren't you answering the phone?!!!"

"Because I don't want to," she spat out to him.

He could smell the wine on her breath. He moved her to the side and walked into the condo. She held the door open in disbelief for a full minute as she took in the fact that he wasn't going to leave. She finally closed the door and followed him into the den.

He was standing near the couch looking into the fire. She felt the tide changing as she saw the look on his face.

"Is everything okay?" she asked.

Uh...yeah. You...how are you? I've been calling you all day. I needed...I mean wanted to see you," he stammered over his words.

"I'm...okay," she said as she pulled him down next to her on the sofa. She grabbed her glass of wine off of the end table and slowly gulped it.

The two sat in silence, staring into the fire. Ten minutes went by before she broke the silence.

"I was in love before. His name was Carter Bradford. He was my everything," she started as the hot tears slid down her face. She took a deep breath and continued, "I was engaged to be married. We were planning to spend the rest of our lives together. Carter was my best friend. He was handsome, kind, caring, intelligent, funny, a giver never a taker, the love of my life. We planned to have babies, to grow old together and raise our family. Shane, he was such a nurturer. He cared about everybody, just like you. He was a protector, a great son and brother and I miss him terribly. Not a day goes by that I don't think of him."

She took a long draw from her wine glass and wiped her face with her hand.

"I told him not to go. I told him to wait until the morning but he wanted to make sure Mike didn't lose the truck, so he went anyway. He called me after they slid off the road the first time..."

Her heart was racing as her memory allowed her to visualize that day a year before. The tears were stinging her eyes and her eyebrows were furrowed and Shane could tell she was no longer there with him. Her body was there with him but her mind had traveled back to that fateful day.

"I told him then to pull over but he kept going and I waited for him to call me back! I waited all day! I waited for him to call me back because he said he would!" she screamed throwing the glass into the fire.

Shane watched her carefully as she stood up and started pacing the floor as she continued her rant with her eyes closed. He let her release her emotions but was watchful that she didn't hurt herself.

"He never called. A police officer called...there was only one survivor...dead on impact," she stuttered out dropping to her knees.

"He promised me that he would be back!"

Shane held her close as he joined her on the floor. She cried into his chest. His eyes were burning with tears that he had held on to for a year. He held her to his chest and rocked her until her crying slowed.

The fire crackled as he lifted her head to look into her crying eyes. He used his thumb to wipe away the tears. The hurt was evident on her face as she lifted to her knees and their mouths joined together like two magnets.

The soft kiss turned into a passionate kiss. Her hands slowly unbuttoned his shirt and pushed it down off his shoulders. He pulled the cashmere sweater that she was wearing over her head.

He cupped her innocent face looking for any sign of hesitation. She reached up and kissed his lips dispelling any thoughts of retreat.

They both eagerly undressed as the fireplace crackled and snapped a symphonic melody. He laid her down on the carpet and delicately traced her breast with his tongue, her back arched as her nipples began to tingle as he manipulated her erogenous zone. She grabbed his broad shoulders as he wandered further down her body landing right at her center.

She gasped as she felt his warm mouth kissing, licking and stroking expertly, quickly bringing her to her first orgasm in over a year. The powerful feeling left her legs trembling as she struggled to recover.

He gave her no grace period as he slipped on the Magnum condom and pulled himself up to penetrate her world.

They worked together grinding like there was a way for them to be any closer than they were. They switched positions ending up with her small frame straddling him. She moved in a melodic rhythm that only they knew. She leaned forward putting her hands on his chest for leverage. That was when she noticed it.

Her finger traced the scar on the left side of his chest and it all started to make sense. She increased her movement as a plethora of emotions spilled over into the situation. He braced himself for what was to come next.

Audrey bent down and kissed his chest, rocking her hips slowly as the momentum was building. She kissed the scar crying harder. Shane was crying too as the moment of realization finally set in. She set back and Shane held unto her hips as they both climaxed at the same time.

She laid her head on his chest and listened to his heart beating. He lied still as she cried into his chest. He wasn't sure if she was going to punch him or kiss him.

"It's his?" she sobbed sitting up and looking deeply into his eyes.

"Yes...I wanted to tell you..."

She quieted him by putting her finger to his lip. She laid her head back down with her head to his chest.

"He promised he would come back," she cried smiling up at Carter. They fell asleep in front of the fire as it crackled and slowly died but not before witnessing the rebirth of an undying love.

Chapter 21

Audrey was totally at peace, not a nervous bone in her body when she heard a tap at the door.

"Come in," she said rising from her seat. The girls had already gone downstairs to line up so she figured it was her time.

"Audrey, are you ready?" Inga said walking into the room.

"As ready as I'll ever be," Audrey said smiling at the woman that everyone else feared but she'd grown to trust and respect.

"I wanted to take these few minutes to say that I am so happy for you. This by far has been the most meaningful wedding that I have ever coordinated," Inga said stepping closer to Audrey and putting her hands on her shoulders. "You are so blessed to have had love transcend even through death. I wasn't that lucky and I now know that no day is promised to you. I live everyday like it is my last and put my all in everything that I do. I may have missed my chance at everlasting love but it would be a travesty if you were to do the same. Honor your husband, Audrey. He is a good man. You deserve the best and I would have to say you got it."

Audrey was so surprised at the heartfelt message from Inga that she stood there in shock. As vague and ambiguous as her statement had been, Audrey took meaning from the message and couldn't think of anything else to do, so she hugged her.

Inga stiffened up as if the 'Old Inga' had warped back into the body that stood before Audrey, but she accepted the hug and even hugged back.

"Thank you, Inga. I appreciate all that you have done for us. You're the best," Audrey said as she took the bouquet that Inga handed her.

"That's what they tell me. Now let's go get married," she said opening up the door and leading Audrey down the spiral staircase that lead to her wedding ceremony.

Reaching the last of the steps, Audrey's bridal party had reached their destination on either side of the altar. Austin awaited her by the grand doors as she began her steps toward him. She could see Shane standing at the altar smiling nervously. Butterflies flew every which way in her stomach until something old caught her eye.

It was Mike, Carter's best friend. Since the accident, she secretly blamed him for Carter's death. Audrey hadn't seen him in years but heard about his condition. Mike had suffered a series of hardships due to the accident. His collar bone was broken in half, his left leg was shattered, and he fell into a deep mode of depression soon after the accident.

Mike couldn't let it go that Carter was dead. He beat himself up about it over the years and carried the hurt and pain with him everywhere he went. He retreated to alcohol to ease his turbulent pains until he wound up in the hospital with alcohol poisoning. That's when he heard about the wedding. That's when he made up his mind to at least do one thing right for Audrey, for Carter.

Audrey stopped in her tracks and looked directly into his eyes. As much as she wanted to hate Mike, she couldn't. She saw the pain in his eyes, in his heart, and in his life. He looked a mess, considering what he used to be like.

He limped towards her without words as the strike of his cane against the floor echoed in the huge foyer of the mansion. Inga quickly intercepted Mike and directed him back out of the door. Mike refused and the noise level began to rise. Heads turned to see what the commotion was about. Audrey ran over carefully holding her dress off of the floor in Mike's behalf.

"Inga, he's okay, he can stay...I-I know him," expressed Audrey.

Inga's raised brow and ice cold blue eyes showed her disapproval but she stepped aside and respected Audrey's wishes.

Trembling, Mike started with, "Au-Audrey, I'm sorry about Carter. I shouldn't have asked him to ride with me. I should have just let him drive and..."

Audrey's heart cried inside as she witnessed Mike's true pain. She sshhd'd him and went in for a hug. Audrey fought hard to hold back her emotions and tears, but in the end, they won her over. Mike stood there off-balanced and made the best of the hug that he could. His unshaven face was flooded with tears as he apologized for Carter's death over and over.

Audrey stepped away, careful to keep Mike balanced on his cane and said, "I blamed you for Carter being gone every night, and...I'm sorry. I'm sorry to have put such a heavy burden on another soul when life is too short in itself. Mike, I forgive you...can you forgive me? Can you forgive me for being so distant, for cutting you out of my life, for not being there for you? Can you forgive me for not being a true friend, as Carter would have been?"

Mike managed to squeak out, "Y-yes..."

Everyone that was seated sniffled or had to wipe their eyes. Audrey told Mike that she loved him and that Carter still loved him as well.

"Audrey, I believe that I held on to this for a reason, and now I know why...here is your something blue." Mike pulled out a teal blue Jaguar key chain, the same key chain from three years ago that Carter had bought for her on the day he perished.

Audrey giggled when she saw the car. "He promised me he would get me one. Hey...this is my something blue!" Audrey hugged Mike once more. "Thank you Mike, thank you so much!"

Inga cleared her throat loudly just after she had wiped away an escaped tear from her own eye.

"Oh Mike, well...I have to get married now. It was so good to see you, thanks again!" said Audrey as she began walking towards the door. Mike stood there in the center of the foyer and watched. Audrey paused in her step and turned back to Mike. She looked back at Austin with the unspoken question in her eye. Austin smiled and gave her the 'ok.'

"Mike, could you... I mean only if you feel comfortable, would you do me the honors, please?" Audrey asked as she held out her arm for Mike to grab. He happily agreed and the two made their way down the aisle...

As the reverend carried on with the ceremony, that same old blue jay found a place on the huge window ledge. It didn't chirp, nor sing, but watched in peace as his love found a new life of love, all the while keeping his heart next to his...forever.

THE END

Please visit:

www.somethingoldsomethingnewcomments.wordpress.com

to post your comments.

Your feedback is appreciated!

Please enjoy an excerpt of the next Erica N. Martin novel to be released

March 2010

Love Crossed Over

Chapter 1

Ramone, just stay where you are and I'll be right there," I said into my earpiece as I pressed the button for the garage door opener outside of the door leading into my kitchen. I threw on the Nike Air Max that sat outside in my garage for occasions like this. My burgundy Range Rover set there purring waiting for me to get in as I'd hit the remote starter on my key ring as I tied my shoes.

I had to go back in as I had forgotten my purse on the kitchenette table. I grabbed the limited edition Gucci cruise bag and was on my way.

I ignored Ramone's 34th phone call because there was really nothing I could do until I got there. I plugged the address he'd given me into my GPS system and waited for the lady with the soothing voice to direct me to my destination.

Twenty minutes later when I pulled into the driveway of Richard Trenton's house my heart dropped. The mansion sat on top of a hill and I wasn't happy to see that my star client had been present at a party that had seemingly gotten way out of control.

Richard Trenton was as notorious on the basketball court as he was for having parties that were "off the hook."

I wasn't surprised to see a sprinkling of other athletes and a few video hoes as I parked and ran into the open doors. My biggest concern was finding Ramone Pratter, first round draft pick in the 2008 NBA draft.

Ramone had just hired me as his agent and no sooner than the ink had dried I was aware of what a task that was going to be. He called me for everything! That was fine with me because under my title as agent came with so many sub-titles, like etiquette coach, contract negotiator, counselor, and mess cleaner upper. I was definitely in "cleaner mode" as I observed everyone that was present at the party.

I walked up the winding staircase and found Ramone, Richard and 3 other men standing in one of the bedrooms outside of the connected bathroom.

"Hey Ms. Bryant," sang Richard in a patronizing way. He was still salty at me for passing up his offer or request for my services. I knew an accident waiting to happen when I saw one and quickly declined. I think he knew to this day that I could have gotten him a much better deal than the 24 million dollar contract he'd gotten. Even the 10% that I would have earned off that contract wasn't enough for me to have to deal with his shit.

Everyone in the league knew I was the best. Money wasn't my motivation because I was financially set. It had taken me 6 years and 10 key deals to be able to pick and choose whom I dealt with. I was a millionaire before I turned twenty-six.

Ramone stared at me with wide eyes not saying a word.

I tried to assess the situation without being completely obvious.

"Hi I'm Sasha Bryant," I introduced myself to the three men that I didn't know.

"Emmanuel Logan," said one.

"David King," the second one said holding my hand a little longer than necessary.

"Jose Delgado," the third man said.

I scratched all three names on a mental notepad that I was keeping.

"She's in there," Ramone said nodding his head towards the door.

"Look I'm telling you now, this bitch better not try that rape shit," Richard spouted out his mouth before I could ask what happened.

"What happened?"

"Nothing. She was doing what she always does and then she started tripping," Richard explained.

I shot Ramone a look and he threw up his hands. I sighed loudly and made my way to the door of the bathroom. I heard a few remarks from Mr. King about the way my jogging suit was fitting my ass. I ignored them and continued on to the door.

I heard whimpering coming from the other side as I knocked.

"Hi sweetie. My name is Sasha and I need you to open the door. I need to know if you are ok. No one else is going to come in with me. I just want to make sure that nothing is wrong with you."

I waited a few minutes and was going to start pleading again until I heard the lock click open. I slowly pushed the door open. She set on the edge of the Jacuzzi tub with her face in her hands. She was butt naked except for a pair of red five inch stilettos.

"Oh Lord," I said to myself.

I slowly walked over to her and she raised her head. I saw a girl that I prayed was at least eighteen. Her face was almost lost in her Beyonce weave but I was able to see that there were no bruises, only smeared mascara.

"Are you ok?" I asked draping one of the massive towels over her shoulders.

"No," she simply replied between sobs.

"Can you tell me what happened?"

"Are you the police or something?" she asked.

"Did you call the police?" I asked avoiding answering the question and attempting to acquire some valuable information.

"No I didn't. My purse and cell phone are in there," she said pointing into the room where my client stood.

"What's your name and what happened in there?"

"My name is Teena. They hired me to dance and...can you help me leave?" she cried.

"Of course, you can leave. I'm sure you weren't being kept here against your will, right?" I asked but at the same time stated trying to guide her answer as the tape recorder in my purse picked up our conversation.

"No, I wasn't. But it got a little wild in there and I got scared. Richard was asking me to do some shit that I don't normally do and he knows I ain't like that. He was really tripping...yelling at me and shit," she explained.

"Wow, really?" I asked feigning concern. I was concerned about her well-being but my biggest concern was making sure I cleared my client. "Was Ramone tripping like that, too?"

"Who is Ramone?" she asked.

"You know the brown skinned tall guy. The one with the curly hair."

"Oh the young cutie," she said with a smile creeping across her face. "Nah, young cutie was the one that was telling Richard to chill out. He just walked in the room, thank God."

I was flooded with relief. Some of my words of wisdom had sunk in at some point. Whew!

She gave me the once over and noticed I wasn't dressed for "partying."

"That must be your man. You all good. I would be checking on his ass too if I were you," she said getting up and tying the towel around her body.

I laughed and said, "Nah, we're just really good friends. Did you drive? Do you need me to call you a cab?"

Her face screwed up as if she had expected me to give her a ride. Shit! I wanted her as far away from Ramone as I could get her ass. I already had his name cleared and I didn't need any other opportunities to arise to pull him back into this shit.

"I'm straight. I drove, but thank you anyway," she said rolling her eyes.

At that point I didn't give a damn how she felt about me. I had the information that I needed, except for one piece.

"Teena, just curious...who hired you to dance tonight?"

"Richard, of course. But he don't have to worry about it anymore. Not for now anyway..."

Chapter 2

"What were you thinking?" I screamed at Ramone through my earpiece as I walked back to my truck. I had to balance on the uneven rocky walkway. I don't know who told Richard that was cute but if I fell and twisted an ankle or something, I'd be suing his ass. "I told you about going to Richard's parties. Some shit is always jumping off, Ramone. You don't need that kind of press."

I peeled out of the driveway back down the hill watching in my rearview mirror for Ramone's headlights to soon follow me.

"I know Sasha. Man, you know how Richard is. He was pressing me to come. I haven't been to any of his shit and him and the rest of the guys were starting to get on me. I was just going to show my face. Man, I was looking for him so we could have a beer and I could be out. Then I walk into some damn madness. My man is going crazy on the chick," Ramone explained.

"Typical Richard," I said relieved that he was now behind me.

"Nah, this nigga had one of his pit bulls in there. He wanted her to let the dog fuck her, Sasha. I thought he was playing but his ass was on some serious shit. The girl was crying so I told him to quit tripping and he looked at me sideways like he wanted to do something to me."

"Ramone."

"I'm just saying Sasha. So the chick got up and ran into the bathroom and I started to leave but I decided to call you to make sure I was in the clear. I didn't have shit to do with this mess and you told me to call you."

"You did good and I'm so glad that you didn't have anything to do with it. For the last time, stay away from Richard Trenton. He doesn't mean you any good. Trust me, I know. You have 4 months until the season starts. Stay out of trouble, or else!" I warned as I turned left on Grant Boulevard and he kept straight to his new home not far from where we'd just come from.

"Yes Mama Sasha. Man, you would think you were some old lady and not just thirty. It's past 12, Happy Birthday Sasha. We need to hook up later. I got you a little something," he said

"Thanks buddy. I'm wise beyond my years little grasshopper. Go home and get some sleep. I'll call you tomorrow," I said hanging up.

I pulled back into my garage at 4:15 a.m. Mission completed.

***

Walking into the bathroom of my master bedroom I put my life in retrospect. I was in tip-top shape. I stripped out of the jogging suit. Washing my face I stared into my own hazel eyes. I stepped back and looked at my slender waist, C cup breast and long legs and smiled. My sandy brown hair hung to the middle of my back and with the blonde streaks I was often described as a prettier Tyra Banks. I thanked the Lord every day for not giving me her forehead!

It was June 12th and I was thirty years old. I ranked amongst the top five most sought after sports agents in the country. This title was earned from a lot of hard work and perseverance. I graduated magna cum laude from Clark Atlanta after playing four years of college basketball and majoring in Sports Management. Everyone including my mother and father thought I would be drafted to the WNBA but that wasn't my dream. I liked being behind the scenes.

I liked negotiating the numbers. That's where my passion lied. I wanted to make the big bucks on the sidelines not on the court. That's not to say that my fortune came with no blood, sweat or tears. I learned a lot on my way to the top. A lot that I will never forget.

I slipped my 5 foot 10 inch frame into a gown and got in the bed next to my boyfriend of a year, Keston Louis.

He mumbled something and moved up to spoon me. His 6"4 frame easily curved around mine and he breathed into my neck. I know he wasn't happy about me getting up at all hours of the night but he knew my job was 24/7.

I realized he was happier to see me than I thought as I felt myself being poked in the back by his hardening penis. He kissed my bare shoulder and maneuvered his way under my gown.

"Happy Birthday baby," he said as he positioned himself to give me one of my presents.

Visit www.secondtimemedia.com for updates and signing dates

Order Form

To place mail orders, please send money orders payable to Second Time Media & Communications LLC to:

Second Time Media & Communications
P.O. Box 401367
Redford, MI 48240

15.00 + tax (MI sales tax 6%) = 15.90

Turnaround time is 3-4 days.

Number of Books _____ x $15.00 _____
Tax _____
Subtotal: _____
Shipping & Handling $2.85 _____

Total: _____

Shipping Information

Name:_____
Address:_____
City:_____ **State:**_____ **Zip:**_____
Contact Number (optional):_____
Email :_____

Your support is appreciated!

Humbly yours,

Erica N. Martin

Something Old...Something New

Order Form

To place mail orders, please send money orders payable to Second Time Media & Communications LLC to:

Second Time Media & Communications
P.O. Box 401367
Redford, MI 48240

15.00 + tax (MI sales tax 6%) = 15.90

Turnaround time is 3-4 days.

Number of Books   _____ x $15.00 _____
Tax   _____
Subtotal: _____
Shipping & Handling $2.85   _____

Total: _____

Shipping Information

Name:_____
Address:_____
City:_____ State:_____ Zip:_____
Contact Number (optional):_____
Email :_____

Your support is appreciated!

Humbly yours,

Erica N. Martin

Printed in the United States
146493LV00001B/2/P